SLEEPING WITH DARCY

A PRIDE AND PREJUDICE INTIMATE VARIATION

HESTER ROSE

Cover image by carlodapino/depositphotos.com

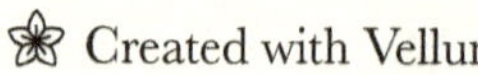 Created with Vellum

CHAPTER ONE

Elizabeth Bennet read a note from her oldest sister Jane at the breakfast table. Jane had gone to Netherfield the day before, but with the heavy rain, she had stayed the night rather than coming home. And now, it seemed that Jane was ill, and she planned to stay with their neighbours until she was well. She wrote that it was only a sore throat and a headache, but Elizabeth suspected that it was much worse. Jane rarely complained and she would not want to be a bother.

Elizabeth folded the note. "I think I should go to see Jane."

Mrs. Bennet said, "Nonsense, I am certain she is fine."

Elizabeth said, "I would still like to go and see her. Papa, may I have the carriage?"

Her father declined from behind a newspaper. "It is needed on the farm."

"It is no matter," Elizabeth said. "I will walk." Longbourn the family home was only three miles from Netherfield Park, and Elizabeth would enjoy the exercise.

"Walk?" Mrs. Bennet repeated incredulously. "How can you be so silly to think of such a thing, in all this dirt? You will not be fit to be seen when you get there."

"I shall be very fit to see Jane, which is all I want."

In the end, it was decided that her sisters Kitty and Lydia would accompany her as far as Meryton, one mile away, and then she would continue on her own.

Lydia and Kitty wanted to call on their Aunt Philips so they could hear all the gossip about the local militia. Currently Lydia and Kitty fell in love every week with a new officer.

Elizabeth had no intention of falling in love – or of getting married – but those were thoughts that she kept private.

As the mother of five daughters and no son to

inherit the family home, Mrs. Bennet was desperate to get them all married as soon as possible. That was why she had sent Jane to Netherfield on horseback the day before when it was threatening to rain. She wanted Jane to stay overnight, so she could spend more time with Mr. Bingley.

Elizabeth did not know what she thought about that. She liked Mr. Bingley well enough for he was amiable and good-natured and was rumoured to have a fortune of four thousand pounds a year. He would probably make an excellent husband for Jane. Jane was amiable and sweet-natured as well. Elizabeth had never heard her say anything disparaging about any of their acquaintances.

Elizabeth, however, was not as good-natured. Many people irritated her, but she had learned to focus on the humour of their oddities. As her father once said, "For what do we live, but to make sport for our neighbours, and laugh at them in our turn?"

Elizabeth thought that this was a wise approach. It was better to laugh than to be angry all the time.

Once Elizabeth was by herself, she lifted her skirts so she could walk faster, even run if she wished. She crossed field after field at a quick pace, jumping over stiles and springing over puddles. She increased her speed as she approached Netherfield, running as fast as she could for several hundred feet, then stopped to catch her breath as she reached the edge of the ornamental gardens.

She gasped for air, enjoying the feel of her heart beating so rapidly that it felt as if it might burst from her chest.

She sighed as her heart beat gradually slowed. She loved to run, and when she was younger, she had run nearly every day, even when it rained. She had also climbed trees and walked along fence railings with no fear of falling. Her father used take her fishing and joked that she was the son he never had, but all that changed when she grew older. As she grew breasts and started her menses, her mother insisted that she abandon her hoydenish ways and dress as a proper young lady.

There was a constant war between her and her mother. Her mother wanted her sleeves and bodices tight, whereas Elizabeth wanted them looser so she could move her arms freely. Elizabeth's happiest times were at the end of the day, when she could slip out of her confining dresses and wear nothing but a loose comfortable shift. She liked nothing better than to lie in bed and read until her evening candle burned out.

Elizabeth straightened her skirts and brushed

the sleeves of her spencer jacket as she approached the large manor house. She saw that her boots were caked with mud and her petticoats were dirty along the hem, but she hoped that her skirt would hide most of it. And if not, so be it. She had come to see Jane, not to impress Mr. Bingley or his odious friend Mr. Darcy.

THAT MORNING, Fitzwilliam Darcy finished dressing and briefly looked out his bedroom window to ascertain the weather. It had rained the night before and he wished to go riding after breakfast, if he could. He was pleased to see that the sky was clear with only a few clouds.

And then he saw her – a young woman with her skirts up around her waist, running at an incredible speed across the lawn. He thought at first that she might be in danger, but as she neared the house, she stopped, held one hand across her chest and let her skirts down.

On closer observation, he realized that it was Elizabeth Bennet.

What she was doing, walking on the Netherfield

lawn at this hour, he could not tell, but he saw that she was now approaching the house.

Why did she not have a servant?

Didn't she know how dangerous it could be for a young woman to travel alone?

And what was she doing, hiking her skirts up that high? He, and anyone else who was looking out at that moment, had a clear view of her legs – a flash of bare thighs and then her white silk stockings that were fastened above her knees.

Damnation, he thought. Did she have no sense of decorum or modesty?

He was horrified, and yes, if he were honest, aroused. Elizabeth Bennet had lovely long legs and for a moment, he imagined running his hands up the back of her knees and onto that cool smooth flesh.

He wondered if her mound was bare under her skirts as well, or if like some of the French women, she wore pantalettes.

But he would not think of that.

Elizabeth Bennet was a gentleman's daughter, not a harlot.

But she had an uncomfortable habit of disrupting and occupying his thoughts. He'd met her a few weeks before, at a local assembly. Initially, he had not been very impressed. She was too short to be a true beauty, and her features were commonplace. But over their next few meetings, his opinion had undergone a radical change.

He noticed that although her figure was not perfectly symmetrical, it was light and pleasing. Her manners had an easy playfulness that was refreshing to him after the conceit of the fashionable world. And her dark eyes, so intelligent, gave her face character, making her more beautiful than he had originally recognized.

He found himself fascinated by her. He watched her every move, listened to every conversation.

Darcy knew it was madness.

Her family position was below his own. Her father was a gentleman farmer with tenants, but his wife had brothers in Trade - one was an attorney in Meryton, the other some sort of merchant in Town.

Darcy did not want to like Elizabeth Bennet. He wanted to have nothing to do with her, and yet, he could not look away from her.

He took a deep breath to compose himself and walked down to the breakfast parlour, where Bingley greeted him. "Good morning, Darcy. I trust you slept well."

"I did," he answered.

Miss Bingley, who had just taken a bite of eggs, smiled at him. Bingley's other sister, Mrs. Hurst was there as well. Her husband, Mr. Hurst, was not. He regularly consumed massive amounts of alcohol and never made an appearance before noon.

Darcy had just sat down with his meal, when a servant announced that a Miss Elizabeth Bennet had arrived.

"Good heavens, what is she doing here?" Miss Bingley said irritably.

Bingley said, "Perhaps she is here to see her sister."

Darcy frowned. "What is this?"

Miss Bingley explained. "Miss Bennet came to dinner last night and with the rain, we thought it best that she spend the night. But now, this morning, I learned that she is ill with a sore throat. She wrote a letter to her mother."

Bingley added, "And we have sent for Mr. Jones."

Darcy could see that Bingley was happy to think of Jane Bennet staying at his house. The night before, he had made a comment about wanting to cut their dinner with the officers short so he might be able to see Miss Bennet before she returned home.

Bingley asked the footman to show Miss Bennet in.

When Elizabeth entered the room, she took Darcy's breath away. Her hair was windblown. Several curls were hanging down across her forehead and one reached her shoulder. Her fair skin was radiant, glowing with health.

She reminded him of Romney's paintings of Lady Hamilton when she was younger. He wished he could commission a painting of her to immortalize this moment. She was beautiful and vibrant, her eyes brimming with intelligence. Her lips were soft, and he wanted nothing more than to kiss them.

Her skirts, which had been up to her waist, were now slightly wrinkled, making him want to wrinkle them further. He wanted to pull her skirts up, cup her buttocks and hold her against himself.

If he were not a civilized man, he would pick her up, throw her over his shoulder and take her upstairs.

But he was a gentleman, so he clenched his teeth and stared at his breakfast plate.

Elizabeth explained that she had come to see her sister.

"Of course," Bingley said. "I understand that she slept poorly and is feverish. You may see her right away, but would you like something to eat first?"

"No, thank you."

Miss Bingley said with a look of contempt, "Did you walk here? All the way from Longbourn?"

"Yes," Elizabeth said.

"But that is four miles!" Mrs. Hurst said, astonished.

"Only three," Elizabeth said. "And I did not mind the walk for it is quite a pretty day."

At this point, Miss Bingley stood and offered with poor grace to take Elizabeth to see her sister. Elizabeth followed her, and Darcy forced himself not to stare at her beguiling backside as she left the room.

CHAPTER TWO

ELIZABETH WAS glad that she had taken the effort to come, for as she had feared, Jane was much more ill than her letter had indicated. Jane was pale and listless, lying in a large four poster bed, too tired to sit upright. She was delighted to see Elizabeth, but she was not equal to much conversation. She coughed and blew her nose.

Elizabeth sat on the side of her bed and held her hand to Jane's hot forehead. "You poor dear," Elizabeth said. Although she did not say it, she blamed her mother for sending Jane out into the rain.

Miss Bingley kept her distance, said she hoped that Jane would feel better soon, and then returned to the breakfast table.

When the apothecary Mr. Jones came, he agreed that Jane had a violent cold. He advised that she stay in bed, drink bone broth and take some draughts he proscribed.

"Can I go home?" Jane asked.

"No, not if you wish to get better," Mr. Jones said solemnly.

Miss Bingley looked annoyed at this but said that Jane could stay as long as she needed.

Later that afternoon, when Elizabeth planned to return to Longbourn, Jane looked sad and said weakly, "I wish you could stay."

At this point, Miss Bingley offered to send a carriage to Longbourn to fetch clothes for both Elizabeth and Jane. "You may stay as long as you wish as well, Miss Elizabeth."

"Thank you," Elizabeth said gratefully, knowing that Miss Bingley did not want either of them there.

At half past six, Elizabeth was summoned to dinner. She stayed only long enough to eat, then returned to Jane. Later, when Jane slept, she thought it best for her to go downstairs to join the rest of the household for coffee.

When she entered the drawing room, she found the whole party at loo, and was immediately invited to join them. But Elizabeth suspected that they might be playing for high stakes, so she declined. She entertained herself by looking at a few books that were laying on the various side tables.

Mr. Hurst said, "Do you prefer reading to cards? That is rather singular."

Miss Bingley made some joke about Elizabeth despising cards.

Elizabeth assured her that she like playing cards as much as the next person, but that she also enjoyed reading.

Darcy said that one of life's greatest pleasures was reading a good book.

Miss Bingley glared at him, and he returned his attention to the card game.

Elizabeth glanced at several books. There was a novel by Fielding that she had already read and a book of poetry that did not interest her. Then she saw another volume behind a cushion on the couch. It was a small book, easily hidden in her hands, with gold and orange on the binding. There was a foreign language on the front cover, possibly Indian.

She flipped through the pages and almost dropped the book from shock. She gasped, but fortunately none of the card players noticed or turned her way.

She returned her attention to the book. It was

full of colour illustrations, showing the most alarming poses of men and women copulating.

Good heavens.

She felt the blood rush to her cheeks.

There was a picture of a woman sitting on a garden bench, wearing an ornate dress, open in front, with her knees apart. A man knelt before her with his face between her thighs, with his tongue reaching for her nether regions.

The look on his face was as if he wanted nothing more than to lick her.

Elizabeth closed the book and looked around the room. Where did this book come from, and who in the room had been reading it? Surely not Miss Bingley or Mrs. Hurst. Could it be Mr. Hurst? Mr. Bingley? Mr. Darcy?

Elizabeth shivered. She had never imagined a man wanting to do such a horrid thing. The thought of a man licking her between her legs was appalling. She shifted, suddenly uncomfortable on her chair.

She told herself that she should put the rude, distasteful book away. She should not look at it. And yet, it remained on her lap while everyone else in the room played cards.

Elizabeth opened the book again, this time to a

picture of a man standing behind a woman. The man cupped the woman's round, bare breasts, pinching the nipples. The picture was drawn from a side view; his large male organ was inserted in the woman.

Good heavens.

Elizabeth closed the book. She had seen dogs copulating before, but she had never thought of people doing the same.

This was what people did when they were married.

This was how babies were made.

Elizabeth quickly put the book back behind the cushion where she had found it and walked away, towards another chair.

As she sat down and picked up a different book, she wondered how it would feel if a man held her breasts and pinched her nipples. She felt her nipples stiffen and she hastily adjusted her shawl to cover the bosom of her thin cotton dress.

With half of her attention, she listened to the conversation at the card table. Miss Bingley talked about the wonderful library at Darcy's home, Pemberley, and she also mentioned that she wished to see Miss Darcy soon. "How I long to see her!" she exclaimed. "I have never met anybody who has delighted me so much. Such a countenance, such manners! And so extremely accomplished for her age! Her performance on the pianoforte is exquisite."

Elizabeth noticed a subtle look of distaste – quickly hidden – on Mr. Darcy's face as Miss Bingley spoke. Elizabeth was amused to see how Miss Bingley desperately wanted to please Mr. Darcy, and yet she was failing miserably.

Miss Bingley wanted to marry Darcy, that was clear, but Elizabeth thought she would not win him with her flattery.

There was some additional conversation about accomplished women. Bingley thought that all the young women of his acquaintance were accomplished, whereas Darcy and Miss Bingley disagreed. Darcy said he did not know more than six women who were truly accomplished.

Elizabeth smiled, saying nothing, and Darcy asked her what her thoughts were on the matter. She said, "I think you must have high standards for what is truly accomplished."

"I do," he admitted. "It is a compliment too readily given and very rarely earned."

Elizabeth said, "I think in general that you are not prone to compliment anyone."

He looked at her sharply and said, "You may be right."

Miss Bingley, not liking them to have a conversation where she was not an active participant, asked if anyone would like to play the pianoforte.

Elizabeth declined and later excused herself to return to Jane.

"You are a most affectionate sister," Bingley said.

"Yes," Darcy said. "Your sister is fortunate to have you."

Was that a compliment? Elizabeth wondered but did not tease him. Instead she merely nodded, saying, "I am the fortunate one," and then said good night.

AFTER ELIZABETH LEFT THE ROOM, it seemed to Darcy as if the evening had lost all its entertainment. He did not want to listen to another song played by Mrs. Hurst or play another game of cards. He wanted to talk to Elizabeth Bennet, but she was not available.

Fortunately, Bingley yawned, and the party soon separated. He and Bingley spent an hour drinking brandy in front of the fireplace, and then finally, it was time for bed.

Once he was in his bedroom, his valet Chetti helped him disrobe and put away his clothing. Darcy donned a silk dressing gown over his night-shirt and dismissed the elderly man. "That will be all."

"Good night, sir," the man said with a bow.

Chetti had been his father's valet for years. He was from a merchant family in India and had moved to England three decades before. He dressed in silk robes and wore a turban on his head. The man was diligent with his duties, but Darcy wondered if it was time to let him retire. But every time he mentioned it to him, the man said only, "I wish to serve until my service is unsatisfactory" and Darcy did not have the heart to let him go.

Darcy read for an hour and meant to blow out his candle, when he heard a strange sound in the hall – a shuffling sound followed by the sound of something falling and a muffled curse.

He opened his bedroom door and glanced into the hallway.

To his astonishment, he saw Miss Elizabeth Bennet, wearing a white cotton nightgown, walking down the hall, towards the stairs. Her hair was down, twisted into a fat braid with curls at the end. Her feet were bare on the hall carpet. It looked as if she had stumbled over a chair in the hallway, for it was now on its side with its legs sticking out.

She carried a candle on a candlestick to illuminate her way.

"Miss Bennet, what are you doing?" he hissed, but although she looked at him directly, she did not answer him.

Her eyes had a glassy stare that made him think that she was sleepwalking. He quickly tied the belt on his dressing gown and followed after her.

His cousin Anne de Bourgh was a sleepwalker, and he knew how dangerous it could be. Once when Anne had visited Pemberley, she had set some curtains on fire in her sleep. Darcy's father had spoken to a doctor about what could be done to help her, and the man said that the best course of action was to shadow her, making certain she did not come to any harm. He was also advised not to wake her. According to the doctor, the best course of action was to encourage her in a calm voice to go back to bed.

His aunt Lady Catherine had been horrified by Anne's actions, and they had quickly returned to Rosings, never to visit again.

Darcy walked behind Elizabeth as she walked slowly down the stairs and across the hall and into the drawing room. She walked directly, with purpose, but for what purpose he could not tell. He hoped she did not want to play the pianoforte. He had heard stories of sleepwalkers doing such things. There had been one man who had even saddled a horse and rode him in the middle of the night. He had woken in the morning, miles away from home, not knowing how he had gotten there.

In the flickering light, Darcy could see the curve of Elizabeth's waist and hips under her nightgown. She was beautiful.

She walked over to one of the couches and set the candle down on a side table. She then withdrew a book from behind an embroidered cushion.

Darcy drew his breath in sharply. It was his book, a gift from Chetti, with excerpts from the Kama Sutra, a collection of Hindu writings. It must have fallen out of his coat pocket. Darcy watched as Elizabeth looked through the book, her face expressionless.

Darcy was horrified, embarrassed, wondering what pictures she was seeing. The book was not meant for young ladies of quality. He approached her and said calmly, "Pardon me, Miss Bennet.

That is my book. Please return it to me." He held out his hand and waited, praying that his words would not wake her.

Elizabeth looked at him as if she was in a daze, but she obeyed him, placing the book on his outstretched palm.

Darcy sighed. "Thank you."

"It is a naughty book," she said clearly. "Most indelicate."

"Yes, it is," he agreed.

"Why do you have such a book?"

Darcy did not know how to respond to that. The book was a gift from his valet, given with the hope that it would encourage him to find a wife. Darcy had thought that Bingley might enjoy it, but he had not shown it to him.

He said, "You are asleep, Miss Bennet, and you should go back to bed."

She frowned. "But I don't want to go back to bed."

Neither did he, actually, but she must get back to her room to avoid scandal. If anyone discovered them alone together in the middle of the night, they would be forced to marry. He said, "Please go back to bed."

Elizabeth nodded slowly and turned to walk out

of the room, forgetting the candle. Darcy followed her quickly, carrying the candle so she could see.

Silently they walked back up the stairs to the wing of Netherfield where they were staying. Darcy's bedroom was on one side of the hallway; Elizabeth's was on the other.

Darcy straightened the chair that she had knocked over.

"Did I do that?" she asked quietly.

"It does not matter."

At her bedroom door, he blew out the candle, because he did not want her to have an accident like his cousin. He stood in her doorway as she walked into her bedroom which was slightly illuminated by the coals in her fireplace. He watched as Elizabeth climbed into the bed. For a moment, her nightgown raised, showing the sweet curves of her leg and thigh. "Good night, Mr. Darcy," she whispered.

He groaned, reminding himself that he was an honourable man and would not take advantage of her incapacity. "Good night, Miss Bennet."

CHAPTER THREE

Elizabeth woke the next morning, feeling remarkably refreshed. She stretched her arms and dressed quickly with the help of one of Miss Bingley's maids. Today she wore a dotted swiss day dress with a high neckline and long straight sleeves. The maid styled her hair in a simple bun, but a few natural curls escaped.

Jane did not seem better, however, and Elizabeth thought that their mother should be consulted. A note was quickly sent to Longbourn and after breakfast, Mrs. Bennet arrived, along with Kitty, Lydia and Mary. Elizabeth was embarrassed to see that all of them had come, but she knew that everyone wanted to see Netherfield. Mrs. Bennet spoke to Jane briefly and then returned downstairs to say that yes, Jane was too ill to be moved. "We must impose upon your hospitality a little longer, Mr. Bingley."

Bingley said, "It is no imposition, ma'am. I am happy to do whatever is necessary to help your daughter recover."

Mrs. Bennet beamed at him. Elizabeth could see that her mother had no real fear for Jane and was happy to have her spend as much time as possible at Netherfield.

Miss Bingley assured her that Jane would receive every attention while she remained with them.

Having dismissed Jane from her mind, Mrs. Bennet now turned her attention to Mr. Bingley's home. She complimented him on his gravel walk, the sweet breakfast room and the charming prospects. "I do not know of a place in the country that is equal to Netherfield. You will not think of quitting it in a hurry, I hope, even though you only have a short lease."

Elizabeth noticed that Mr. Darcy looked pained at her mother's expressions. Whether it was the effusion of her compliments or the fact that she, like everyone else in Meryton, knew so much of Bingley's business, Elizabeth did not know.

Darcy, sensing her observation, said quietly, "Miss Elizabeth, I hope you are enjoying your stay at Netherfield."

"I don't know if I could say that I am enjoying it precisely, considering the fact that my sister's illness is the cause, but I am very comfortable, thank you."

"Did you sleep well?"

He looked at her intently, as if he truly cared about her answer.

Elizabeth said, "Yes, sir. I slept very well."

Mrs. Bennet overheard their conversation and added, "Thank goodness for that! I had my concerns when I learnt that you were going to stay the night, Lizzy."

Elizabeth frowned slightly and her mother explained to the rest of the room that when Elizabeth was younger, she had often sleepwalked. "But only when she was particularly tired, or if she slept in a new place. I remember the first time you slept at my brother's place in Gracechurch Street. You wandered out into the street in the middle of the night and we didn't find you until the morning. You were asleep on the front steps. It was a miracle that you weren't hit by a carriage." Mrs. Bennet clasped her hands over her ample bosom. "You can imagine how my poor heart fluttered. I was never the same afterwards. That is the pain of motherhood, Mr. Bingley. A mother never rests because of the worry she has for her children."

"That is alarming," Darcy said. "What was done to protect her?"

"Oh, to be certain, we locked the doors, and as far as I know, she didn't escape again."

Elizabeth was embarrassed by all the attention she was receiving. She said, "I believe sleepwalking is more of a childhood behaviour. I haven't slept walked for years."

Miss Bingley sniffed in a superior manner. "That sounds positively frightening. I am glad to say that I have never sleepwalked."

"How would you know?" Darcy asked pointedly. "I understand that the victims rarely remember their nocturnal wanderings."

Elizabeth said, "I believe it is like dreams. I remember very few of mine."

Bingley said, "I remember many of my dreams when I wake, but by the time I am dressed, I have often forgotten them."

"That is a blessing," Darcy said dryly. "I believe there is nothing more tiresome than listening to someone recount a detailed dream that fascinates the dreamer but is tedious to everyone else."

Elizabeth said, "Perhaps Mercutio was correct, and Queen Mab gives us dreams particularly tailored to our own desires."

Bingley nodded, "That is Shakespeare, correct? *Much Ado about Nothing*?"

"No," Darcy said bluntly. "*Romeo and Juliet*."

Mrs. Bennet sighed, "So romantic. Such a wonderful play."

Elizabeth said, "I believe the play is a warning." A warning to never fall in love.

"Yes," Mrs. Bennet agreed. "They should have never married without their parents' consent."

"Or at least been less eager to kill themselves," Darcy said dryly. "Half an hour's reflection and restraint on either of the young lovers' parts would have altered the story completely."

"That would never happen to you, Darcy," Bingley said. "You are too methodical."

"That is better than being impulsive."

Elizabeth considered Mr. Darcy from the corner of her eyes, noticing his formal stance and the rigidity of his jaw. She thought Bingley's assessment was apt. Mr. Darcy would never be like Romeo, reciting poetry at midnight under a young woman's balcony. She smiled as she imagined such an improbable scenario.

Bingley said, "Perhaps I am impulsive. I remember when I made the decision to rent Netherfield." He snapped his fingers. "It was a matter of hours, not days. And I do not regret it."

"No, indeed. It was a very good decision," Mrs. Bennet said. "Speaking for the neighbourhood, I can assure you that we have all been blessed by your decision."

Again Mr. Darcy looked pained and turned away.

At this point, Lydia spoke up, reminding Mr. Bingley that he had once promised to host a ball. "It would be the most shameful thing in the world if you did not keep your promise!"

Elizabeth was mortified by her pertness and saw Miss Bingley glance at her sister and raise her eyebrows meaningfully. No doubt Darcy was appalled as well, but Elizabeth could not see his face.

Bingley was more gracious, however. He said that he was perfectly ready to host a party as soon as Jane was recovered. "For you would not wish to be dancing while she is ill."

Elizabeth wasn't too certain of that. Lydia and

Kitty lived for enjoyment, wanting parties every night. Lydia often complained that life at home was dull unless there were officers around.

Elizabeth was relieved when her mother and sisters finally left. She excused herself and went upstairs to spend the morning with Jane rather than having to speak with Bingley's sisters or Mr. Darcy.

IT WAS clear to Darcy that Elizabeth did not remember sleepwalking the night before. He could not tell her because he did not want to embarrass her, or worse, set up a situation in which he would be forced to marry her, so he kept silent.

When Elizabeth was not present, Miss Bingley teased him about Mrs. Bennet, implying that she would soon be his mother-in-law. Miss Bingley did this because he had once made the mistake of telling her that Elizabeth had fine eyes, and she wanted to torment him.

But Darcy did not need Miss Bingley to remind him of how miserable a union between himself and Elizabeth would be.

He would enjoy lying with her, that would be a

pleasure, but having to visit and converse with her family would outweigh any conjugal benefit.

Mrs. Bennet was as scheming as every other matchmaking mama that pursued him in London, but she had less finesse. She was vulgar and common. He didn't know why Bingley didn't pack his bags and leave Netherfield before he found himself leg-shackled to a Bennet.

And the younger Bennet girls – Darcy could never remember which one was Lydia and which one was Kitty – were beyond correction.

They flirted outrageously and were so loud.

He hated to think of his sister Georgiana following their example.

Because of this, he would keep his distance from Elizabeth.

But every time they were in the same room, he found himself glancing at her, waiting for her to speak, then listening to her conversation.

He tried to occupy himself with writing a letter to his sister. Miss Bingley stood by him, pestering him with questions, admiring his handwriting, saying that he wrote quickly, offering to mend his pen, asking him to tell his sister that she longed to see her. Darcy found Miss Bingley irritating and wished that she would take a hint – that he did not want to marry her and that no amount of flirtation and flattery would change his mind.

Indeed, as much as he enjoyed Bingley's company, Darcy thought he might have to avoid him in the future if Miss Bingley was always underfoot.

He noticed that Elizabeth, unlike Miss Bingley, did not draw attention to herself. Instead, she busied herself with sewing or glancing at books.

Later in the evening, when Miss Bingley played some Italian songs on the pianoforte and followed them with a lively Scotch air, Darcy drew near to Elizabeth and said, "Do you not feel an inclination to dance a reel, Miss Bennet?"

She smiled slightly but made no answer.

He repeated the question, surprised by her silence.

"Oh," she said. "I heard you before, but I did not know what to say. I knew if I said yes, that you would despise me for my common taste."

"No, I could never despise you." The moment the words left his mouth, Darcy regretted them. He did not want her to know the strength of his infatuation.

Elizabeth said, "Besides, we would need more people if we were to dance a reel."

Bingley, overhearing them, said, "Louisa and I could join you."

"No," Miss Bingley said sharply, suddenly ending her song. "I am too tired, and it is too late. I have played too long. If Miss Bennet wishes to play, she may follow me."

Elizabeth declined graciously. "No, you are right. It is getting late and I should go back upstairs to see Jane."

Bingley said, "Yes. Do tell your sister that we are praying for a quick recovery."

Elizabeth smiled at him and Darcy wished that smile was for him. She said good-night and soon left. As he watched her walk away, Darcy wondered if she would sleepwalk again, and if he had been remiss not to warn her.

CHAPTER FOUR

DARCY WOKE from a sound sleep to see Elizabeth standing beside his bed, staring down at him. He sat up, alarmed. "Hell's bells. What are you doing here?"

Elizabeth frowned and tilted her head slightly as if she was pondering his question. Just like the night before, her eyes were glassy. She wore a nightgown, but this time, it was not buttoned all the way to the top. There was a triangle of her décolletage showing in the faint light from the fireplace. Tonight, she did not carry a candle.

Her beautiful dark hair fell around her shoulders. She was a vision of beauty that would torment his dreams. She said finally, "I don't understand you."

Darcy climbed out of his bed and quickly donned his dressing gown, hastily tying the sash. "I don't understand you, either, Miss Bennet. You should not be in my room." He took her arm to gently guide her back across the hallway to her own bedroom, but then he heard footsteps in the hall, and he froze. "Don't speak," he whispered.

He did not want anyone to know that she was in his bedroom.

Together they stood in silence, waiting for the footsteps to quieten.

She rubbed her cheek against the sleeve of his dressing gown, and he flinched, pulling away.

"Soft," she protested and turned towards him, running her hands down his arms. "So soft."

He took a step backwards so she would not discover that another part of him had become very hard. When he spoke, his words were choked. "Please, Miss Bennet. You don't know what you're doing."

She smiled at him, with a lazy, sleepy smile that made his blood pound. Although he knew it was wrong, he wanted to kiss her. He wanted to press his lips to hers and plunge his tongue into that sweet mouth.

She said, "Miss Bennet is my sister. I am Miss

Elizabeth." She spoke petulantly, like a child, but she was all woman as she stood before him.

"You must go back to your room," he repeated. He reminded himself that she was half-asleep and not responsible for her actions.

She traced a paisley design on the chest of his dressing gown with one finger, making him shake. "Where is your book?"

It was currently hidden beneath his mattress. "It is not for you."

"Why not?"

"It is not for young women." Not gently raised young women such as herself. He tried to catch her finger to keep her from touching him, but when he did, she stepped closer to him and looked up at him, all soft and kittenish.

"Kiss me?"

He stiffened. "No." Darcy never knew that he had such great discipline.

She stood closer so that her breasts brushed against him and he gasped.

She said, "Just one kiss. Please? I have never been kissed before and I would like to understand it."

Darcy groaned. "You are asleep and don't know what you are doing."

"Please?" She lifted her chin and closed her eyes.

Darcy was not a saint. He caught her up in his arms, reached down and kissed her lips softly.

She sighed and opened her sleepy eyes. "That was nice, but not remarkable. Is that all there is?"

Darcy's masculine pride was wounded. He kissed her again, this time pressing his lips more urgently against hers. Her hands clutched his arms and she gasped.

Unable to stop himself, he teased his tongue into her mouth.

Instead of recoiling, she opened her mouth, accepting his tongue, caressing it with hers and sucking on it.

Dear sweet heaven. Darcy's head swam. He kissed her again and again, plunging his tongue into her mouth.

She writhed, clutching at his arms, his shoulders, rubbing herself against him as if she could not get close enough.

He kissed her neck, under her ear, her throat.

She panted, "Oh, that is much better."

One of his hands was behind her, on her waist, pulling her close and the other palmed one breast over her cotton gown, rubbing against that sweet mound of flesh as he nuzzled her throat. He felt her nipple as hard as a pebble and he fumbled for the buttons on her nightgown to free her breasts.

She moaned and that sound seemed to wake him.

Damnation. What was he doing?

Darcy stepped back, dropping his hands to his sides.

She frowned, reaching for him. "What is wrong?"

He said stiffly, "You must go back to you room." He would not ruin her.

Elizabeth sighed. "Will you come with me?"

"No." As much as he would like nothing better than to come with her, he could not. He took her hand and tugged on it, leading her to his door.

She pouted but didn't resist him as he walked with her from his room to hers. Again, he watched as she climbed into her bed. "Good night, Miss Bennet."

"Call me Elizabeth," she said huskily.

He clenched his hands into fists, holding himself back. "Good night, Elizabeth."

She sank down on her pillow with a happy sigh. Her white nightgown shifted, baring one beautiful smooth shoulder. "Good night, Fitzwilliam."

Darcy swallowed. He would like to hear his name on her lips for the rest of his life. But that was madness.

He carefully closed Elizabeth's door and tiptoed over to his room. Once alone, he lit a candle and pulled out his book of pictures. He imagined Elizabeth in the various poses: Elizabeth warm and willing, lithe and supple, accepting his aching cock.

He imagined her draped in silks and dripping with jewels, breasts bare, lying back in her bed, looking at him with passion in her eyes.

He shut the book closed with a snap. He was a fool.

THE NEXT FEW days at Netherfield passed slowly. Elizabeth was bored. There was nothing to do but take care of Jane, sew, read, and take walks. Normally, she would enjoy verbally sparring with Mr. Darcy, but he seemed distant and more quiet than usual. He complained of a headache and retired to bed early.

Elizabeth slept poorly that night. She woke once, confused, finding herself standing by her bedroom door which for some reason would not open. She supposed she needed to use the chamber pot, did so, and returned to bed. In the morning, her door opened easily. She asked the girl who laid the fire in the morning if the door had been locked during the night, and she said, "No, miss."

Jane gradually improved and the next day, she was able to spend the evening with the rest of the company. Bingley was most attentive, making certain she had ample shawls and that the fire was built up. He sat beside her, smiling and talking with her the entire time. He looked besotted.

Darcy sat by himself, reading a book, saying little, but Elizabeth noticed that he was often watching Bingley as well.

Miss Bingley, irritated by the lack of conversation, asked Bingley, "Are you seriously considering having a ball?"

Bingley beamed. "I am," he said and turning to Jane, he added, "And I hope to have the first two dances with you, if you will have me."

Jane blushed and said, "I will."

Miss Bingley said, "Not everyone considers a ball to be a pleasure. To some of those among us, a ball would be a punishment."

Bingley said, "If you mean Darcy, he may go to bed if he chooses before it begins."

Elizabeth glanced at Darcy to see his response to his friend's teasing. She expected him to be offended, or at least irritated, but he looked amused instead. "No, do not worry. I will be at the ball," Darcy said. "And I will dance with each of the ladies present tonight, starting with you, Miss Elizabeth, if you would do me the honour."

Everyone looked at her, Miss Bingley glaring, all of them waiting for her answer.

She gave a little nervous laugh. "I cannot promise. Who knows what will transpire between now and then? There must be a date set and a true invitation given. You may ask for a dance on the night of the ball, Mr. Darcy, not before."

His eyes seemed intent upon hers. He said, "I will do so."

She thought his answer most odd, considering the fact that the night they met, he had declared her not handsome enough to dance with. She had overheard him conversing with Bingley at an assembly several weeks before, and since then, she had not liked Mr. Darcy at all. He was too proud, too arrogant, and considered himself above his company.

But now, it seemed that his opinion of her had changed.

Or was he merely being polite?

She frowned. Mr. Darcy was not known for his politeness.

No, he seemed to be blunt to a fault, saying what he wished without caring what anyone else thought.

Did that mean that he truly wished to dance with her?

Elizabeth did not know what to think about that. She was glad that Jane was getting better and they would be able to return to Longbourn soon.

CHAPTER FIVE

Mrs. Bennet was not happy to see Jane and Elizabeth return from Netherfield – she had hoped that they would stay at least a week – but she was mollified to learn that Mr. Bingley would be giving a ball soon. "Jane, you will need a new gown," Mrs. Bennet announced. "Something that will make Mr. Bingley declare himself!"

As Mrs. Bennet busied herself with ribbons and laces, Mr. Bennet announced over breakfast that his cousin Mr. Collins would be visiting.

"Mr. Collins!" Mrs. Bennet cried. "What is that evil man doing, coming here?" She clutched her hands over her bosom. "My heart is racing. Tell me you are joking, Mr. Bennet. Tell me that you would not allow that viper into this house."

"He is not a viper," Mr. Bennet corrected. "From what I understand, he is a clergyman now."

Elizabeth smiled, amused by her father's dry humour.

But Mrs. Bennet was not amused. She wailed, "But when you are dead, he may throw us out!"

"That is true," Mr. Bennet admitted calmly as he buttered his toast. Everyone in the household knew that Mr. Collins was his heir and upon Mr. Bennet's death, Mr. Collins would inherit Longbourn.

Mrs. Bennet cried, "How can you torment me? I hate Mr. Collins and I hate the entail! If I had known that your estate was entailed upon another, I would not have married you!"

"And if you had given me a son, ma'am, Mr. Collins would not inherit."

"Oh, oh," Mrs. Bennet cried. "How can you be so cruel? Didn't I try for a son? Seven times I nearly died, bringing your children into the world."

Elizabeth knew that in addition to her four sisters, there had been two more girls who had been born too early and died soon afterwards.

Childbirth could be dangerous, another reason for Elizabeth to avoid marriage.

Mrs. Bennet continued, "And we would have had more, if the doctors had not advised against it."

Elizabeth looked down at the breakfast table, wishing that her parents did not fight in front of their children. From her perspective, both were at fault, and nothing was gained by washing their dirty laundry in public. Her poor mother might be silly and hysterical, but her father was dismissive and at times, unkind.

Mr. Bennet said, "Dry your tears, Mrs. Bennet, for Mr. Collins comes offering an olive branch. He wants to marry one of our daughters."

With these words, Mrs. Bennet brightened. "Did he say that exactly?"

"He implies it. He wrote that he wishes to make our daughters every possible amends."

Mrs. Bennet said, "Well then, perhaps I don't hate him after all." She thought for a moment and said, "He can't have Jane because I want her to marry Mr. Bingley. But he could have any one of the rest of you girls."

Elizabeth was horrified by her mother's attitude – that any man was welcome to any of them, as long as he would inherit Longbourn. "I am in no hurry to marry, Mama," Elizabeth said.

Lydia giggled. "I want to marry a soldier, but I

might change my mind if Mr. Collins is very handsome."

Kitty agreed.

Mary said that she would have to meet him first before making a decision.

Mr. Bennet excused himself from the table, saying that they were all silly, ignorant girls.

Unfortunately, when Mr. Collins arrived that afternoon, he was not handsome. He was a solemn, heavy looking young man of five and twenty. His manner was grave and stately, and his manners were very formal. He bored them all by talking about his patroness Lady Catherine de Bourgh.

And, having taken Mrs. Bennet's advice, he centred his romantic attentions on Elizabeth, who tried to avoid him as much as possible.

The next day, when Lydia wanted to walk to Meryton, Mr. Collins joined her, and at the last moment, Elizabeth said that she wished to stay at home with Mary. When the walkers returned, Elizabeth learned that the party had briefly met Mr. Bingley and Mr. Darcy who came to Meryton on horseback. Also, Lydia and Kitty had made the acquaintance of a handsome new soldier named Mr. Wickham. "And Aunt Philips promises to invite him to dinner tomorrow night, so you can all meet him!"

Elizabeth was not interested in meeting any more soldiers, no matter how handsome they were, and the next night, she held herself back from the conversations. Rather than play cards, she glanced through the books in her aunt's bookcase, finding nothing of interest.

Not that she expected her aunt to own a copy of the book she had seen at Netherfield, Elizabeth thought wryly. She often thought of the pictures she had seen, wondering if all married people did such things.

She could not help but imagine various married couples in the depicted positions: Sir William and Lady Lucas, her Aunt and Uncle Philips, her parents.

She shivered, not wanting to think of her parents doing such things. But she knew that since her mother had given birth to seven children, they must have done something similar at least seven times.

As he had promised, Mr. Bingley invited them all

to a ball the following Tuesday. Mrs. Bennet was flattered that Bingley and his sisters made an effort to invite them personally, rather than merely sending a card. Elizabeth was glad that Mr. Darcy had not joined them on their visit. She did not like the way he often stared at her, frowning.

No doubt he was cataloguing all her flaws.

As they prepared the ball, Lydia talked about dancing with Wickham. "I shall dance every dance with him!" she said as she twirled around.

"You cannot," Elizabeth said. "Unless you are engaged, you may not dance with a gentleman more than twice in one evening."

"Oh pooh," Lydia said. "No one cares about those old-fashioned rules, anymore."

Jane said, "If you don't obey the rules, people will gossip about you."

Lydia said, "I don't care."

Mary said, "You will care if your reputation is ruined. A woman's reputation is no less brittle than it is beautiful, and we cannot be too much guarded in our behaviour towards the other sex."

Lydia pouted. "Very well. I will only dance two dances with him, but I think you are all very mean. You don't know what it is to be in love."

Jane blushed but did not comment.

Elizabeth was concerned about Lydia. She spoke to her privately and asked her if she was falling in love with Wickham.

"I am," Lydia said staunchly. "And Wickham is falling in love with me."

"But you have only spoken to him a few times."

"People can fall in love in an instant," Lydia argued.

Elizabeth thought of Romeo and Juliet. She said, "It isn't wise, Lydia. What do you know about him?"

Lydia said, "He told me all about himself. His father was a steward for Mr. Darcy."

"Mr. Bingley's friend?"

"No, his father. Old Mr. Darcy. And old Mr. Darcy was Wickham's godfather. He treated him like a son, paid for his schooling, and wanted him to become a clergyman."

"Like Mr. Collins?"

Lydia nodded. "And I think he would have been a marvellous minister, but when old Mr. Darcy died, the present Mr. Darcy was horrid. He refused to grant Wickham the living. That's why he became a soldier."

Elizabeth was astonished. She did not like Mr.

Darcy, but she did not think him capable of such evil. She said, "That is terrible."

"I know," Lydia said. "But that is the way of the world. Wealthy men can do whatever they wish, and humble, hard-working men like Mr. Wickham suffer."

Elizabeth said, "Please be careful, Lydia. I don't want you to break your heart. It is unlikely that Mr. Wickham is in a position to take a wife." She thought that Lydia was too young to fall in love.

Lydia shrugged. "I can take care of myself."

That evening, after they arrived at Netherfield, Lydia came up to Elizabeth and said unhappily, "He's not here."

"Who?"

"Mr. Wickham."

"I thought Mr. Bingley was going to invite all the officers."

"He did," Lydia said. "But Mr. Denny says that Wickham chose to go to Town on business, instead. Because he wanted to avoid that nasty Mr. Darcy."

"Perhaps that is for the best," Elizabeth said. If the two men had a quarrel with each other, perhaps they should avoid each other.

"I wish I could go home," Lydia said. "There is no point in staying now."

Now Elizabeth was truly concerned. Lydia did not sound like herself. She said, "Don't let Wickham's absence upset you. Look at all the other officers in their red coats. Surely one or two of them are worth dancing with."

Lydia nodded. "You are right. And perhaps when Wickham returns, he will hear what a grand time I had and be jealous."

Elizabeth shook her head sadly as she watched Lydia skip off to find Kitty and some eligible red coated dance partners.

"Miss Bennet, may I have the honour of the first two dances?"

Elizabeth turned to see Mr. Darcy standing before her. She knew he was tall, but now that he was standing so close, he looked even larger in his dark coat and cream coloured breeches. His shoulders were broad and the white cravat at his throat was perfectly pressed. He was every inch the gentleman.

She took a deep breath, ready to decline the invitation, when Mr. Collins interrupted.

"Dear Cousin! Miss Elizabeth!" he said. "I believe I have the first two dances."

Elizabeth looked guiltily at Mr. Darcy. "It is

true, Mr. Darcy, he does. He asked me several days ago."

"And I asked you before that," Darcy reminded.

"Good heavens," Mr. Collins said, turning towards him. "Are you Fitzwilliam Darcy, the nephew of Lady Catherine de Bourgh?"

Darcy looked at him coolly. "I am."

Mr. Collins said, "It is an honour to meet you, sir. I am Mr. Collins, recently her ladyship's minister and she speaks of you often."

Elizabeth could tell that Darcy was offended. As the man of superior situation, it was his right to determine the nature and depth of their interaction, and it was clear that he did not wish to converse with Mr. Collins."

Mr. Darcy said, "Which is it to be, Miss Elizabeth – are you going to dance with me or your cousin? The music has started."

Elizabeth thought it likely that Darcy would be the better dancer, but she had made a promise to Mr. Collins.

Mr. Collins bowed low. "No, sir, I insist that you dance with Miss Elizabeth first. I will gladly take your seconds."

Elizabeth was offended. Did she have no say in

the matter? She felt somewhat like a bone between two dogs.

And if there was a fight, she knew that Darcy would win. Not only was he several inches taller, he had a natural athletic grace that made her think he may have done some boxing in his past.

She liked the image of him knocking Mr. Collins down with a well-placed facer.

Mr. Collins continued. "Indeed, my dear, when we are happily united, I know that you will often be required to dance with others, and it will be my pleasure to share you."

He bowed and scraped again.

Elizabeth wanted to punch him herself.

When Darcy offered her his arm she took it, if only to separate herself from Mr. Collins.

CHAPTER SIX

DARCY CLENCHED his hands into fists and then relaxed them as he walked onto the dance floor. He was surprised by how irritated he was. He was furious by Mr. Collin's behaviour. Not merely by his introducing himself like a vulgar bore, but more by his assumption that Elizabeth would one day belong to him. As he and Elizabeth stood in line, waiting for the other pairs of dancers to go down the row, Darcy asked, "Are you engaged to Mr. Collins?"

She startled. "No. Absolutely not," she said quickly.

He nodded, relieved. "But he thinks that you will soon be?"

Elizabeth rolled her eyes. "Believe me, sir. I have

given him no encouragement. But my mother thinks it would be a good match. Longbourn is entailed and he will inherit when my father dies."

Darcy said, "I can see that would be advantageous to your family, but surely not to you personally."

"No, indeed not," she said with a rueful smile. "Mr. Collins and I would not suit. If I had to see him every morning, I would be tempted to poison his breakfast tea."

Darcy was more alarmed by the prospect of that dull man in her bed, his thick body crushing her delicate one as he rutted with her. Every fibre and sinew of his being protested, but he knew he could not stop it.

If he did not want to marry her, she was free to marry someone else.

Even that toad.

ELIZABETH KNEW that Mr. Darcy did not enjoy dancing, but he seemed particularly angry that evening. He frowned as they danced, saying nothing. She was tempted to start a conversation, just to torment him, but decided not to.

She was annoyed with him as well. If he didn't want to dance with her, why had he asked her?

His actions were incomprehensible.

He was an enigma.

But as the music played and she went through the steps, she gradually calmed. She loved to dance, and she would not let Mr. Darcy ruin her evening.

She loved the music played by a small orchestra, and the room was beautiful. It was lit with dozens of standing candelabras and decorated with greenery and swaths of pink fabric. Miss Bingley might be an irritating snob, but she did know how to plan a party. Elizabeth knew that her mother was busily counting the number of wax candles, estimating the cost, and congratulating herself, thinking of all the parties Jane could give once she was married to Mr. Bingley.

As for herself, Elizabeth was wearing one of her favourite dresses – a lovely gown of pale yellow with gold trim around the wide square bodice neckline and in vertical stripes on her puffed sleeves. She wore new long white satin gloves that came up past her elbows. Her curly hair had behaved itself – for once – and it was arranged in an ornate style on top of her head with a few dainty ringlets by her ears.

She wore a simple gold chain with a small cross,

a gift from her Aunt Gardiner, and she had dabbed some rose scent across her throat.

She felt as if she looked her best, and if that wasn't good enough for odious Mr. Darcy, she did not care a whit.

Darcy did not think he had ever seen Elizabeth look more beautiful. Her skin was smooth and soft in the flickering candlelight. He admired the curve of her eyebrows, the sparkle in her eyes, the slight uptilt of her charming little nose, and those rose coloured lips.

Those lips that he wanted to kiss.

Did she ever dream of him, he wondered. Would she ever remember kissing him?

He felt like a cad for having kissed her when she was half asleep, but she had asked him.

As they danced, he imagined himself whisking her out the glass doors and onto the Netherfield lawn and beyond that, to the ornamental gardens.

There in the moonlight, would she protest if he kissed her again?

He forced himself to look at her face instead of

down at her dress and the perfect orbs of her breasts. Like most of the young women present, the neckline of her dress was low, and the bodice was small, following the fashion introduced by the French. Some women hid their assets behind a layer of lace, but tonight, Elizabeth's bosom was a creamy bounty, pert and lifted, no doubt resting as if on a shelf created by a small corset under her yellow gown. He imagined himself unlacing that corset and having her breasts fall firm and round into his waiting hands, then told himself to behave himself.

He was a gentleman.

She was a gentleman's daughter.

But as they danced and her breath quickened, he glanced downward, amazed that her areolae were still hidden by the gold braid of her gown.

She was breathtakingly beautiful.

THEY DID NOT TALK as they danced. Elizabeth saw Darcy glancing briefly at her bosom, and then away as if it did not interest him.

Odious man.

Jane had breasts that looked like a statue of Venus – small and perfectly shaped. Hers were larger and heavier. Did Darcy think they were vulgar? Elizabeth wondered if she should have tucked some lace into her neckline, but she found that lace was often scratchy, and she did not like to wear anything uncomfortable.

She had a sudden thought of her in a shift with Mr. Darcy's hands on her breasts, cupping them, rubbing them like one of the pictures in that book.

Good heavens.

Where had that thought come from?

Elizabeth felt her face flush and she faltered, missing one of her steps.

Darcy caught her arm. "Are you all right?"

She nodded, too embarrassed to look him in the eye, and quickly found her place again.

Her breath was unnaturally fast.

After a moment, he said, "I met your sisters the other day in Meryton. I was surprised that you were not with them, because I know how you like to walk."

"I do," she said. "But not that day."

"I hope you were not feeling poorly."

That was polite of him, which surprised her. He

had some manners, apparently. "No," she answered. "I am in excellent health."

"I am glad to hear it. And your sister, too, she seems to be completely recovered."

Elizabeth glanced over at Jane who was dancing with Bingley. "Yes, she is well."

Again they were silent, and Elizabeth thought that would be the extent of their conversation, but then Darcy added, "That day in Meryton, your sisters were speaking with some officers."

Elizabeth narrowed her eyes. Was he going to say something about her younger sisters and their flirtatious behaviour?

He said, "I know one of them. His name is George Wickham, and I would recommend that you and your sisters be on guard against him."

Elizabeth said, "Whatever do you mean?"

"Do not trust him."

"Good heavens," she said. "You cannot drop that pronouncement without explaining yourself."

Darcy said, "Perhaps I should have said nothing, but I cannot bear to think of you or anyone you care about being harmed by him."

"Harmed? I understand that you are the one who harmed him."

"Is that what he told you?"

"No," she said. "I haven't even met the man, but my sister Lydia told me that –"

He interrupted. "Your sister should be careful."

What an arrogant, bossy man. If there was one thing Elizabeth hated, it was a man who thought he knew better than everyone else.

Elizabeth was relieved that the music had stopped, and their dance had now ended. She stepped away from him, saying, "You are presumptuous, sir, to tell me who can be a friend to me or my sisters."

Darcy said, "Wickham is no friend to any woman."

He spoke with such assurance that for a moment, Elizabeth was stunned. She then said, "It is not your place to school me."

He stood for a moment as if struggling with his thoughts, wanting to say more. But finally, he bowed and said, "You are right, Miss Bennet. Forgive me. I meant well."

He then turned and walked away from her.

Elizabeth walked over to a table where there was punch and pastries. She sipped on a cup of punch to calm her nerves, and Charlotte Lucas joined her. Charlotte was a neighbour and Elizabeth's closest friend. At twenty-seven, she was seven years older than Elizabeth and Mrs. Bennett thought she was too plain to ever catch a husband, but Elizabeth valued her honesty and her loyalty.

Tonight Charlotte was dressed in a peacock blue gown with a neckline as low as Elizabeth's. Elizabeth noticed that her gown did not have any lace in the bodice, either.

"I was surprised to see you dance with Mr. Darcy," Charlotte said. "I thought he did not like dancing."

"I don't think he does," Elizabeth said. "And my guess is that he will like it even less now."

"Why do you say that?"

"We argued."

Charlotte was alarmed. "About what?"

"Does it matter? The man is infuriating. High-handed. Overbearing."

Charlotte tsked her tongue. "Do not be a simpleton, Eliza. He singled you out. That was a compliment. You should have used that time to your advantage."

"To my advantage? In what way?"

"To make him like you. To make him want to marry you."

Elizabeth laughed. "You are ridiculous, Charlotte."

"No, you are the ridiculous one," Charlotte said quietly. "The man is worth ten thousand pounds a year. You should have smiled and looked up at him with adoring eyes –"

Like Miss Bingley? Elizabeth thought.

"– rather than arguing with him."

Elizabeth said, "That would be fine advice if I wanted to marry him. But I don't."

Charlotte said, "Sometimes I think you don't want to marry anyone."

That was true, but Elizabeth did not want to admit it out loud. She saw Mr. Collins approach them and groaned.

"What is it? Are you ill?" Charlotte asked.

"No. It is my cousin here to claim the next two dances."

Charlotte looked at him from head to toe. "He is nothing compared to Mr. Darcy, but he will still inherit Longbourn."

Elizabeth said, "I can't dance with him. Not now. I am in such a mood; I would say something reprehensible."

"Would you like me to take your place?"

"Would you?"

Charlotte nodded. "Yes, I'll do it."

Elizabeth gave her a quick little hug. "Thank you, so much. Let me know how I can repay you."

"I will think of something," Charlotte said dryly.

CHAPTER SEVEN

Considering himself under obligation, Darcy dutifully danced with Miss Bingley and Mrs. Hurst at the ball, and then he retreated, staying on the outskirts of the ballroom, observing rather than participating. He watched Elizabeth, naturally, and was pleased to see that she did not dance with Mr. Collins. Her friend Miss Lucas took her place.

Darcy wished he could tell Elizabeth more about Wickham, but he knew she would not believe him.

And did he really want to tell her that Wickham had tried to run away with his own sister Georgiana?

Even now, Darcy wished he had challenged the

man to a duel and shot him through his treacherous heart.

At supper, Darcy overheard Mrs. Bennet talking with Lady Lucas, telling her that she expected Jane to be married to Mr. Bingley within two months, possibly sooner. "Mr. Bingley is such a charming young man, and so rich, and I consider it the greatest comfort that they will only live three miles from us. I couldn't bear it if my daughter married a man who took her away from me."

"What about Elizabeth and Mr. Collins?" Lady Lucas asked.

"Oh yes, Lizzy will be in Kent once she marries, but she will visit, I am sure." Mrs. Bennet lowered her voice and Darcy leaned closer to hear every word. "And if the truth be told, Lizzy is my least favourite. She has always been difficult. Even as a child, she had a will of her own. She was always running about, climbing trees and other nonsense. You remember how I could never keep her dresses clean."

Lady Lucas nodded. "Such a trial. My dear Charlotte was always tidy."

Mrs. Bennet patted her hand. "What a comfort she will be in your old age, able to care for you when all your other children have married and moved away."

After this conversation, Darcy paid more detailed attention to Bingley and Jane Bennet. It was obvious that Bingley was infatuated, but Darcy had seen him in love before. He did not think it would last. And as for the eldest Miss Bennet, she seemed to be a pleasant, good-natured girl, but she did not look at Bingley with any particular affection. She received Bingley's devotion with a calm, detached air that made Darcy think that she did not love his friend and that her heart would not easily be touched.

Unlike Elizabeth Bennet who seemed to be a warm, honest person, even fiery when she disagreed with him, Jane Bennet was more reserved and appeared cold-hearted. Darcy had seen this characteristic before. Sometimes the most beautiful women were also the most unsympathetic and selfish.

Darcy had no qualms about separating Bingley from his current infatuation. Indeed, he would be doing his friend a favour. Bingley was still young and somewhat naïve; it would be good for him to wait until he was thirty to marry. And when he did choose a bride, he deserved a woman who truly loved him as well as a better mother-in-law.

The party ended well after midnight, and the Bennets were the last to leave. Mrs. Bennet tried to invite Bingley to a family dinner, but he said that he would be leaving for London for business the next day.

"When you return, then," Mrs. Bennet said eagerly. "I insist that you dine with us."

"I will do so," Bingley assured her.

And Darcy would do his best to delay that plan.

As the Bennets finally left, he saw Elizabeth yawn and cover her mouth with her gloved hand.

He thought of her wandering about Netherfield in her nightgown and decided that he would call on Mr. Bennet in the morning.

The following day, he called at Longbourn after breakfast, desiring to meet with him privately.

Mr. Bennet looked up as Darcy was announced. "This is unexpected, sir."

"Yes, I know it is, but I must speak to you on a matter of some delicacy."

"Please, take a seat."

Darcy sat in the chair across from Mr. Bennet. He cleared his throat. "You daughter Elizabeth recently spent several days at Netherfield Park.

During that time, I discovered her sleepwalking in the middle of the night."

Mr. Bennet said, "Oh, no. We had hoped that she had outgrown that behaviour."

Darcy said, "I was not alarmed, because once of my cousins is similarly afflicted. I merely escorted Elizabeth back to her bedroom and saw that she was safely back in bed. I did not want to wake her for fear of the repercussions."

Mr. Bennet took a deep breath. "I thank you for your kindness and discretion."

"But that is not all. She came to my bedroom the following night."

Mr. Bennet raised one ironic eyebrow. "And now you wish to make my daughter an offer of marriage?"

Darcy did not find humour in his situation. "No, sir, I do not. I mean no disrespect to you or your daughter, but when I marry, it will be my choice – to a young woman equal to me in fortune and position. I am merely warning you that you must keep better care of your daughter if you wish to maintain her reputation and your family honour."

Mr. Bennet looked at him closely, eyes

narrowed. "What happened when my daughter was in your bedroom? I must know."

Darcy met his gaze directly. "Very little."

"What does that mean – very little?"

Darcy felt a twinge of guilt. "I kissed her, but that was all." He took responsibility for his actions and would not blame it on her.

"Did she wake?"

"No, sir. And as far as I can tell, she has no memory of our meetings."

Mr. Bennet nodded thoughtfully, then said, "Tell me the truth, sir. Is my daughter still a virgin?"

"Yes, sir."

"You know that I can summon a doctor to examine her this morning?"

"Yes, sir. And my answer will not change."

Mr. Bennet stared at him for a moment, as if weighing his integrity. "Very well," he said finally. "If what you say is true, I thank you for your restraint."

Darcy said stiffly, "I am not a man who would take advantage of a young woman incapable of rational thought."

"No, I can see that. I mean no insult."

"Thank you."

"And I appreciate your candour. A lesser man would not have said anything."

Darcy had considered keeping his silence, but at the ball, he knew he must say something. He said, "I admire your daughter and I wish her well. I felt it was my duty to warn you."

"But you don't want to marry her?"

It pained him to be so blunt, but he must tell the truth. "No, sir, I do not."

Mr. Bennet said, "I understand. A man can kiss a pretty woman without wanting to marry her. I made the mistake of marrying below my station twenty-four years ago. Would that I had your wisdom. I don't wish the misery of an unequal match upon anyone."

Darcy nodded, grateful that the man understood.

Mr. Bennet said, "And as much as I adore my daughter, I don't want her to marry a man who does not value her."

His words stung. Darcy knew that he did value Elizabeth, more than he could say, but he was a man of the world. He knew that she would not be accepted by those in his social sphere.

Their differences would draw them apart, making both of them unhappy.

"Thank you, sir."

ELIZABETH WAS SURPRISED to see that Darcy called on her father. They spoke for a few minutes and then he left, bidding them all a good day and farewell. He seemed to look at her for a long moment, and then he was gone.

At this point, Mr. Collins asked Mrs. Bennet for a private audience with Elizabeth.

Elizabeth tried to discourage him, saying that there was nothing he could say that could not be said in front of her mother.

But Mrs. Bennet disagreed and promptly took Kitty with her, leaving Elizabeth alone with her solid cousin.

"My dear Miss Elizabeth," Mr. Collins began. "You can have no doubt as to the nature of my address. Indeed, my attentions have been too marked to be mistaken."

Elizabeth wished to nip his proposal in the bud, so she interrupted him, saying, "Yes, I have noticed your marked attentions and I had hoped that my lack of encouragement would prevent my having to refuse you, but unfortunately my feelings on the matter were apparently mistaken."

Mr. Collins sputtered. "I don't understand. I am proposing marriage."

"I know. You referred to our union last night, which was presumptuous, because I never said I would marry you."

Mr. Collins said, "You don't understand. My patroness Lady Catherine de Bourgh wants me to marry. She said that a clergyman must marry. Lady Catherine told me to choose properly – to choose a gentlewoman for her sake, and for my own, she suggested that I marry an active, useful sort of person, not bought up high, able to make a small income go a good way."

"Excellent advice," Elizabeth said. "But I am not that woman."

"I disagree. You are precisely that woman. Your wit and vivacity may have to be tempered when you are in Lady Catherine's company, but other than that, I believe that you will make me very happy."

Elizabeth felt some sympathy for the man because he was so oblivious. She said clearly, "You don't understand. You will not make me happy. That is why I cannot and will not marry you."

"But – But – I came to Hertfordshire specifically to get engaged!"

For a moment, Elizabeth feared that he might burst into tears. She said, "Then I suggest that you find another young woman – someone other than myself – to marry."

"But whom? How?"

"That is not my decision to make, Mr. Collins." She thought that her sister Mary might find him agreeable, but she would not suggest her – for that seemed unkind.

Mr. Collins said, "Miss Elizabeth, I beg you to reconsider. Do not be hasty. My situation in life, my connection with the family de Bourgh and that fact that I will one day inherit this house, make me highly desirable. And given your small dowry and the limitations of your social sphere, you might never receive another offer of marriage. Don't you think that marrying me is better than becoming an old maid?"

Elizabeth let out a brief bark of laughter. She could not help it. She quickly regained her composure, however, and said, "Forgive me, sir. I appreciate the honour of your proposal, but I must respectfully decline."

She then turned and left the room. Mr. Collins

tried to follow after her, but she held up her hands and said, "No, sir, do not repeat yourself. My answer is 'no.'"

Mrs. Bennet, overhearing her pronouncement, cried out, "Lizzy, are you mad?"

CHAPTER EIGHT

The next few months were difficult for Elizabeth. Although her father was glad that she had refused Mr. Collins, her mother could not forgive her. And to make matters worse, Mr. Collins followed Elizabeth's advice and found another young woman to marry – Charlotte Lucas. Two days after proposing to her, he had proposed to her friend.

Mrs. Bennet said that Charlotte was a conniving false friend. "I shall never speak to her or her mother again!" – which vow she kept for several days.

Elizabeth was astonished as well. She thought her friend was too wise to marry a fool like Mr. Collins, but as Jane reminded her, "Everyone is different. We all value different qualities in a husband."

Elizabeth supposed that at twenty-seven Charlotte had decided that she would rather marry than be an old maid.

Personally, Elizabeth was looking forward to becoming an old maid. She had hoped that she might be able to live with Jane and Mr. Bingley one day as a maiden aunt, but Mr. Bingley remained in London and his sisters and Mr. Darcy left Netherfield to join him. Elizabeth did not know if they would ever see Mr. Bingley again.

When Christmas passed with no news of the Bingleys' return, Mrs. Bennet decided that Jane should visit the Gardiners in Gracechurch street for the winter months. Mrs. Bennet's hope was that if Jane was in London, too, Mr. Bingley might see her.

January was a grey, miserable month for everyone at Longbourn, made even worse for Lydia with the news that Mr. Wickham was engaged to Miss King, an acquaintance of theirs who had recently inherited ten thousand pounds.

"It's not fair!" Lydia cried. "If I had ten thousand pounds, he would marry me."

That was most likely true, Elizabeth thought. She had met Mr. Wickham by this time but had not been impressed by him. Once Darcy had left Meryton, Wickham was eager to talk about their history. Elizabeth recognized that Darcy had harmed him, but she also remembered Darcy saying vehemently, "Do not trust him," so she did not believe Wickham entirely.

Elizabeth was surprised by how often she thought of Darcy. Sometimes when she woke in the morning, she felt as if she had dreamt of him, but the details of her dreams were fleeting.

It was as if they had discussed something of importance that she could not now remember.

But she laughed at her frustration, refusing to be alarmed. Dreams were often strange and should not concern her.

Charlotte married Mr. Collins in mid-January, and at the wedding breakfast, she invited Elizabeth to visit her in Kent in March. "My father and Maria are coming, and I would love to see you as well."

Elizabeth was not certain she wanted to see Mr. and Mrs. Collins as a newly married couple, but with Jane gone and her mother constantly criticising her for refusing Mr. Collins, it seemed a better alternative.

If nothing more, she would have the opportunity of taking long walks in new surroundings and finally meeting Lady Catherine de Bourgh. Elizabeth enjoyed meeting new people and learning their foibles; she highly doubted that Lady Catherine was a paragon that Mr. Collins had described.

DARCY ATE BREAKFAST at Rosings Park, half-listening to/half ignoring his aunt Lady Catherine de Bourgh recite all the news of the neighbourhood. Lady Catherine was interested in everyone's doings and was not hesitant to give advice. She talked about her clergyman, Mr. Collins, recently married to a Miss Lucas. Lady Catherine said that Mrs. Collins was not pretty, but that she seemed to have a good head on her shoulders; she was not giddy or foolish like so many young women these days.

Darcy mentioned that he had met both Mr. Collins and Miss Lucas when he was in Hertfordshire in the autumn.

"What were you doing there?" Lady Catherine demanded.

"Visiting with my friend, Charles Bingley."

Lady Catherine sniffed. "I don't know the Bingleys."

Since Bingley's grandfather and numerous uncles were in Trade, Darcy thought it unlikely that Lady Catherine would wish to know them.

Lady Catherine continued, "The Collins's have company at present. Mrs. Collins' father, Sir William Lucas, a sister Maria Lucas and a friend, a Miss Elizabeth Bennet."

Darcy nearly choked on his toast. "Miss Bennet?"

His cousin Colonel Fitzwilliam noticed his discomfort and said meaningfully, "Did you meet Miss Bennet in Hertfordshire as well?".

Darcy glared at him to keep him quiet. "I did," he said simply.

"Is she pretty?" the Colonel asked.

Darcy felt a surge of annoyance rise within himself. He knew his cousin was baiting him. "She is a handsome young woman," he said casually, not willing to admit that she was the handsomest young woman of his acquaintance.

Lady Catherine's eyes narrowed. She said, "Miss Bennet is too short to be a classical beauty, but she is not unattractive. And she seems intelligent, although she expresses her opinions very decidedly for so young a person."

Darcy smiled, wondering what Elizabeth said that had offended his aunt. Elizabeth's bold truthfulness was one of the things he liked best about her.

In the past few months, Darcy had often thought of his nocturnal meetings with Elizabeth and his decision to leave Hertfordshire. He wondered if he had made the right choice to distance himself from her.

Since returning to London, he was bored and out-of-sorts. He realized that no other woman was Elizabeth's equal.

He wanted to see her again, if only to see if his memories of her were accurate. He hoped that when they met again, she would be like all the other silly, grasping young women of his acquaintance, and he could easily forget her.

Lady Catherine continued to talk, telling them about Elizabeth's family and the fact that her family home was entailed upon Mr. Collins. She turned to her nephew. "I don't think you will find her a suitable marriage prospect, Richard."

As the second son of an earl, the Colonel

needed to marry an heiress if he wished to maintain his standard of living.

Lady Catherine did not consider Darcy a potential suitor for Miss Bennet, because she thought he would eventually marry her daughter Anne. Anne de Bourgh was a quiet, slim woman with poor health who rarely spoke.

Even now, she sat at the breakfast table, daintily eating her oatmeal and eggs, saying nothing.

Anne had been more gregarious in her youth, but over the years, she seemed to shrink, becoming gradually more childlike. Darcy did not know if this was due to her chronic colds or if she could not compete with her mother's more abrasive manners and had given up trying to express herself.

From prior conversations, Darcy knew that Anne did not wish to marry him, just as he did not wish to marry her. He hoped that in time, his aunt would abandon her plans for them.

"I like Miss Bennet," Anne said suddenly, surprising them all.

So do I, Darcy thought and made a decision. "I should call on the Collins's. It is the proper thing to do, considering the level of our acquaintance."

The Colonel smirked. "I will come with you."

ELIZABETH HAD SPENT a fortnight with the Collins's, enjoying the opportunity to converse with her friend again. They spent most of their days in the kitchen or in a separate sitting room, avoiding Mr. Collins who spent most of his time working in the parsonage garden or visiting Lady Catherine.

Elizabeth could see that Charlotte was happy with her choice, but it was not a life that Elizabeth would have chosen for herself.

They were both sewing one morning when a servant announced Mr. Darcy and Colonel Fitzwilliam.

Charlotte said quietly, "Eliza, I think you are the reason for this civility. Mr. Darcy would never have come so soon to wait upon me."

"Nonsense," Elizabeth said quickly, then schooled her face to show no reaction when Mr. Darcy came into the room.

He was taller and even more handsome that she remembered. He was an impressive sight in his buckskins and boots with his broad shoulders and square jaw. She thought his dark hair was longer than it had been before, betraying a tendency to curl. There was one errant curl on his forehead that made her fingers itch to smooth it back.

He bowed and paid his compliments to Mrs. Collins and herself. He then asked their permission to introduce his cousin, Colonel Fitzwilliam.

Colonel Fitzwilliam, not as tall nor as handsome as his cousin, was about thirty and well mannered. He was quick to smile and converse, unlike Mr. Darcy, who held himself stiffly.

After an awkward silence, Darcy did ask about the health of her family.

Elizabeth assured him that they were all well. She then said, "My sister Jane has been in Town for the past three months. Have you ever happened to see her there?"

From Jane's letters, she knew that was unlikely. Miss Bingley had called on Jane in Gracechurch Street only once, and Jane had not seen Bingley at all.

Darcy appeared confused for a moment, then said that no, he had never been so fortunate as to meet her sister.

That seemed to be the entirety of his conversation, however, and after a few more minutes, the gentlemen went away.

Elizabeth returned to her needlework, jabbing

the needle into the cloth. She did not understand herself. For one moment, she had been surprisingly pleased to see Mr. Darcy, and then she was irritated that he was so formal in his address. She wished he would go away, so she never had to think of him again.

CHAPTER NINE

A FEW DAYS LATER, after a particularly violent rain-storm, Mr. Collins informed Lady Catherine that a tree had fallen on the parsonage roof, damaging it and making most of the house inhabitable. Mr. Collins took full responsibility for this act of God, wringing his hands and saying that he should have trimmed the tree earlier.

Lady Catherine agreed and asked him if he would still be able to conduct services on Easter in two days.

Mr. Collins assured her that there would be no problems, no problems at all. He would hire someone to cover the holes in the roof until they could be repaired.

"Take care of it, Mr. Collins," Lady Catherine

said irritably. "And see that you are properly dressed in the future. You look positively unkempt this morning."

"Yes, ma'am," he said, grovelling. "There was no hot water this morning, but that is no excuse."

"No, it is not," Lady Catherine said.

Darcy, having overheard this conversation, later suggested to Lady Catherine that she invite the Collins's and their guests to stay at Rosings.

"Why ever should I do that?" Lady Catherine said. "It would be most inconvenient."

"It would be an example of charity," Darcy said. "Like the Good Samaritan."

Lady Catherine considered the matter and finally agreed that it was her Christian duty to help them.

That afternoon, Darcy looked out one of the windows, watching as one of Lady Catherine's carriages arrived with the Collins's and their belongings. Colonel Fitzwilliam joined him, saying, "Ah, the beautiful Miss Bennet will soon be under the same roof."

Darcy looked at him sharply. "You find her beautiful?"

The Colonel shrugged. "As a work of art only. You know where my proclivities lie."

Darcy nodded. He had known for years that his cousin preferred men rather than women, which was considered scandalous and could be punishable by death if he was caught. Darcy said, "I like Miss Bennet more than I should."

"Why do you say that?"

Darcy sighed. "You have not seen her family. Her mother is vulgar. She has almost no dowry. Her uncles are in Trade."

The Colonel said, "Do not be a fool, Darcy. If you want her, marry her. Do not let anyone else's opinion stop you from finding your happiness."

Darcy looked at his cousin. The man was right, and he should count his blessings. Although some people might disapprove of his choice, Darcy was able to marry Elizabeth if he wished, whereas the Colonel could never marry another man.

"I will do it," Darcy said. "I will propose."

"When?" his cousin teased.

"As soon as possible."

THAT NIGHT, Elizabeth took more time as she prepared for bed. She brushed her hair and braided it, thinking over the evening's entertainment. She had not wanted to come to Rosings, but with the Parsonage in a state of chaos, it had seemed prudent. She was grateful to sleep in a warm, dry bed that night and to know that there would be hot food for breakfast.

For their first evening at Rosings, they had eaten a fine meal – Lady Catherine's cook had created nearly two dozen dishes for their enjoyment. Elizabeth thought the amount of food on the dining room table was extravagant, but she assumed that the servants would eat whatever remained.

After dinner, she had spoken with Mr. Darcy, asking him if he thought Mr. Bingley would return to Netherfield.

Mr. Darcy looked uncomfortable and said he did not know his friend's plans, but that he would not be surprised if Bingley chose to give up Netherfield entirely. "For he seems quite happy in Town. He has many friends and engagements there."

His comments upset her because she knew Jane would be heart-broken if she never saw Bingley again.

Then later that evening, Elizabeth played the pianoforte at Lady Catherine's request and Colonel Fitzwilliam offered to turn the pages for her. Darcy walked across the room to observe them both.

He had a sombre expression, and Elizabeth wanted to provoke him, so she said, "Do you mean to frighten me, Mr. Darcy, by coming in all this state to hear me? But I will not be intimidated, even though I know that you are accustomed to hearing much better music than I can provide."

Darcy said, "I have no intention of intimidating anyone and I have enjoyed your playing every time I have heard it."

That compliment took her aback and she had not known how to answer him.

Afterwards, Lady Catherine said that she would play better if she practised more and could have the advantage of a London master. "And while you are staying here, you may practice on the pianoforte in Mrs. Jenkinson's room. You will be in nobody's way there in that part of the house."

Elizabeth had glanced at Darcy to see his reaction to this statement and saw that he looked ashamed of his aunt's ill breeding.

"Please wake up, Fitzwilliam."

Darcy stirred and opened his eyes to see Elizabeth standing beside his bed. As before, she was wearing a white nightgown and nothing else. There was a lit candle on a table near his bedside. "How did you get here?" he demanded as he sat up. At Netherfield, their bedrooms were across the hall from each other, but at Rosings, her room was in a different hall.

Her eyes had a glassy gaze, but her lips gave a little smile. "I walked."

"I can see that," he said. "But it is unsafe. What if you had walked into someone else's room?"

"I did. I went first to Colonel Fitzwilliam's room."

"Hell's bells," Darcy said. "What happened?"

Elizabeth looked confused. "Nothing. He was asleep, I think."

"Did he wake?"

She shook her head.

Darcy supposed he should be thankful for God's tender mercies. He reached for his dressing gown which lay across the end of his bed, but she pulled it towards herself, keeping it out of his grasp.

"Give that to me," he ordered. "I must take you back to your bed and I won't traipse around Rosings in my nightshirt."

She smiled and shook her head. "Not yet. I want you to kiss me first."

Darcy groaned, then laughed at himself and their situation. "Fine," he said. "You may kiss me all you want, because I am going to marry you. And we can deal with whatever scandal tonight brings."

He held his arms open wide for her. She dropped his dressing gown and climbed up onto his bed.

She reached for him and kissed him on his lips, pushing her tongue into his mouth, startling him with her boldness.

She was obviously a woman who knew what she wanted, and Darcy was not going to hold back. He kissed her, his tongue dancing with hers, his hands rubbing over her shoulders and down her back, drawing her closer.

She burrowed, nuzzling her face against his neck. Her hand reached into the neck of his nightshirt. "You are hairy," she said with wonder as she stroked his chest.

He quickly undid her buttons and then his hand reached into the neck of her nightgown. "And you are not," he teased.

She giggled and that little laugh warmed his heart. What a joy it would be to be married to her, to be able to do this for the rest of their lives. He cupped her breast, loving the feel of her smooth warm skin, the texture of her areola and her stiff-ening nipple.

Elizabeth gasped.

"Do you like that, darling?" he asked. He kissed her again and rubbed his finger over and around the tip of her breast.

"I do," she said when her mouth was free. "Could you pinch it? Just a little."

He did as she asked, and she writhed against him. "Yes, just like the picture," she moaned. "Again. But both, if you please."

Her tone was prim and proper, as if she was asking for another cup of tea. He smiled, thinking of his little book. "Are you thinking of a particular picture?"

She nodded and pulled at her nightgown, sliding it off her shoulders and her arms, suddenly baring her breasts.

Merciful heavens; she was magnificent.

"Pinch both of them," she said.

Darcy had never thought that he would want a woman to order him about in bed, but he was willing to do whatever Elizabeth wanted. "As you wish, Mrs. Darcy," he said and pinched her nipples with both hands.

She moaned and arched her back. "Not Mrs. Darcy," she said firmly.

"Not yet," he promised. "But soon."

He continued to address her breasts, twisting her nipples, then kissing them, first one and then the other, sucking their tips into his mouth until she was panting. "Yes," she breathed out and clutched at his head.

Never had a woman inspired such a passion in him. He looked her directly in the eyes and said, "What now? I am yours to command."

She hesitated and then said, "You might not like it."

"Trust me, I will like it."

She said, "Your tongue. Down here," and reached between her legs.

CHAPTER TEN

Never had a man more reason to be grateful for a woman who liked to read. "Yes, ma'am," Darcy said reverently. "I will be happy to oblige." He climbed out from his tangled sheets. He lifted Elizabeth and turned her so that she was lying down, facing him, her head against his pillow. He then lifted the hem of her nightgown, baring her lovely legs. He kissed each of her knees. "Not there," Elizabeth said impatiently and tugged at his hair.

He did not let her hurry him. He lifted her nightgown higher and rubbed his hands on her thighs before separating them gently.

She drew her breath in sharply, but she did not push him away.

In the flickering candlelight, he could see her

beautiful pubic mound, lightly covered with curling hair. "You honour me," he said.

"Your tongue," she ordered.

Darcy had a moment's doubt. Was he a scoundrel for not waking Elizabeth? The doctor had said that it was best to accommodate a sleep-walker, but had there ever been a situation such as the one in which he now found himself?

If he woke her, she would be frightened. She might scream and there would be hell to pay.

But, he reasoned, if he was going to the devil, he might as well take her with him.

"As you wish," he said and leaned forward.

He kissed her mound and then gently touched her folds with his fingers. She was already damp.

She clutched at his shoulders, letting him know that she liked what he was doing.

He licked his fingers, separated her nether lips and then found her pearl, the little button above her slit. He touched it softly, rubbing it as he had earlier rubbed her nipples – over and around, lightly brushing over the top of it. It stiffened slightly.

She sighed and said, "That is very nice, but it is not your tongue."

"No, it's not," he agreed. He teased her pink flesh with his fingers, slipping one into her quim –

she was wet now – and then brought his mouth down to her. He licked her with one wide swath across her opening and up to her pearl, then back again.

She groaned and he swirled his tongue around her pearl, teasing her with its tip. He listened to her breathing to see what she liked, what touches made her heart race, what made her hands clench.

She pulled at his hair as he continued to work on her, stirring her passion. Never had he cared more for a woman, wanting her to find joy with him. As with most men of his class, his prior sexual acts – which had been few in number – had been with professional women in reputable brothels. The women had acted as if they were pleased by him, but he knew they only cared for his money.

But now, with Elizabeth, he wanted her to be swept away by desire.

He kissed her again and again, licking and sucking, enjoying the sweet, salty nectar that was hers alone.

Her fingers dug into his scalp, but he did not mind. He would not care if she snatched him bald as long as he could have her like this.

He licked her again and again, making her body tense. He tapped his tongue on her pearl. She shivered and moaned quietly and then suddenly she cried out, her entire body jolting.

"Shh," he said, kissing her again. "We don't want to wake the house."

For a long moment, she shuddered, her breath at first in gasps, but then gradually her breathing softened and she relaxed. She looked at him, her eyes smoky and satiated. "Thank you, Fitzwilliam," she breathed out.

"You're welcome," he said, although he felt as if he was the one who should thank her. She had given him a gift, one that he could never forget. "And now, it is time to take you back to your room."

"Can't I stay here?" She rubbed her hands on his chest, over his nightshirt, as if she did not want to let him go.

He put his hands over hers to still them. "No, Elizabeth, you cannot," he said firmly.

Darcy didn't know if he could take her back without being discovered, but he had to try. She pouted as he helped her slip her arms back into her nightgown and then buttoned her buttons, but when he tugged on her hands and said, "Let's go," she followed him docilely out of his room and into the hallway.

WHEN ELIZABETH WOKE the next morning, she thought at first that Darcy was in her bed.

Good heavens, she thought, sitting up in alarm – where was she? This room was unfamiliar, the wall papers strange, but then she remembered that she was at Rosings.

And she was relieved to see that she was safely alone. There was no man in her bed. Darcy was just a dream.

Thank heavens.

She imagined Darcy's hands on her. His mouth on her.

She gasped, placing her hands on her hot cheeks.

It was like something out of that rude little book.

She should never have looked at it, since it gave her such wicked ideas.

But then before she could remember any more details of the dream, there was a gentle knocking at her door. "Come in," Elizabeth said warily.

It was a maid, asking if she would like coffee or chocolate before she dressed.

"Tea," Elizabeth said firmly. There was nothing like a cup of tea to settle her mind.

After tea, Elizabeth dressed and went downstairs for breakfast. She was determined to act with calm decorum. She refused to be embarrassed by a dream.

DARCY WATCHED Elizabeth closely at breakfast, but it appeared as if she did not remember anything of what they had done the night before.

Part of him could not believe it himself. If it was a dream, it had been the best dream of his life, but he did not imagine the marks on his scalp where Elizabeth's fingernails had bruised his skin.

And Chetti had looked at him oddly when he picked his rumpled dressing gown off the floor.

Darcy wondered if the garment smelled differently, possibly picking up some of Elizabeth's intoxicating scent.

The sooner he could propose to Elizabeth and take her home to Pemberley, the better.

After breakfast, Darcy sought out Anne to talk with her. She was sitting by a window, hands in her lap, looking out at Rosing's lawn. Her companion

Mrs. Jenkinson was also there, working on some embroidery. "Anne," Darcy said. "I want your opinion on a book. Would you please come with me to the library?" He held out his hand to her.

"Certainly," Anne said simply as she rose to her feet. There was no emotion in her voice.

Once they were alone in the hall, Anne said quietly, "What is the trouble?"

He was surprised by her question, and she said wryly, "I may not speak often, but I still have eyes. I can tell that something is troubling you."

Darcy nodded. "It is Miss Bennet."

Anne smiled briefly. "You love her."

He raised one eyebrow. "You are observant. I hope your mother hasn't noticed as well."

Anne said, "My mother sees what she wants to see."

Together they walked into the library and found some high-backed chairs. Darcy sat across from Anne and addressed her. He said bluntly, "Miss Bennet is a sleepwalker."

"Then I am sorry for her."

He leaned forward. "And I need your advice."

"Are you thinking it would be a risk to marry her? Is that what bothers you? Do you think she is going to burn down Pemberley?"

"No," he said quickly. "I am not worried about that. I merely wish to know how to take care of her."

Anne said, "You could follow my mother's example and keep her locked up at night, giving her increasingly large doses of laudanum to keep her docile."

"Hell's bells," Darcy said. "Is that what she's done to you?"

Anne shrugged. "It is my life and there is nothing I can do to stop her. She is my mother and my jailer."

Darcy was horrified. He reached out to touch her hand. "Let me help you."

Anne shook her head. "There is nothing you can do. I have tried to reduce the dosage countless times, pretending to take my medicine, but then spitting it out, but when I do, I can't sleep, I have terrifying nightmares, and I feel as if my skin is crawling with maggots."

"Good God. There must be something that can be done."

Anne said, "One of these days, I will find a way to take a greater dosage and sleep forever."

"No," Darcy said, shocked. "You can't kill yourself."

Anne said, "I know killing myself is a sin, but I think the Lord will understand. And if He does not, I shall have to find friends in hell." She smiled wryly. "I have never had friends before. When I was younger, my mother thought no one was good enough for me, and now, no one wishes to speak with me. I don't blame them. I don't have anything of interest to say."

Darcy said, "I can't believe I never noticed how you are suffering. I am sorry that I have done nothing to help you, but I can help you now."

"What can you do?"

"I can take you away from here. I will find doctors to help you."

Anne sighed wearily. "The only way my mother will let me go is if I am married. And since you do not want me, I shall remain a spinster, living as I do now, until I gather the courage – and sufficient laudanum – to end it all."

Darcy did not know what to say. Anne sounded so hopeless. He said, "I will find a way to help you."

She said, "I appreciate the offer, but I know you can do nothing." She smiled briefly. "But enough of that. You did not come to talk about my troubles. You want to tell me about your Elizabeth Bennet. I like her. She is pretty and full of life."

That was one of the things he loved about her. He said, "I have heard that it is best not to wake a person who is sleepwalking."

"I agree," Anne said. "When I have been woken, it is terrifying and embarrassing. It is better for me to wake naturally."

"Do you remember what you have done when you are sleepwalking?"

Anne said, "As far as I know, I haven't slept walked in years, but when I was younger, sometimes I would remember bits and pieces, like pieces of a puzzle. But no, most of it I didn't remember. I certainly don't remember setting the curtains on fire."

Darcy said, "So what should I do to help her?"

"Does she sleepwalk often?"

"I don't think so. From what her mother said, it occurs primarily when she is tired or in a new setting."

Anne said, "Has she slept walked here at Rosings?"

Darcy nodded. "She came to my room last night."

Anne gave a little laugh. "Poor man. No wonder you are terrified. If my mother learned of that, she would throw the girl out. Or set up a guillotine in the morning room."

Darcy smiled as well. "I know. I consider it a miracle that I was able to return Elizabeth to her bedroom last night without anyone being the wiser."

"That was fortunate," Anne agreed. She added thoughtfully, "You should take her away and marry her as soon as possible. Once she is at Pemberley, you can sew bells on the hems of her nightdresses and have footmen posted outside her bedroom doors.

Darcy squeezed her hands gratefully. "I will do that. Thank you."

CHAPTER ELEVEN

As Elizabeth walked around the gardens at Rosings, she met Colonel Fitzwilliam who said he was making his annual tour of the grounds. "Would you care to join me?"

"I would be glad to," she said, and they walked for a while in silence. She asked if he and Mr. Darcy planned to leave Kent on Saturday.

"Yes, if Darcy does not put it off it again. But I am at his disposal. He arranges the business just as he pleases."

Elizabeth thought that comment was interesting, and she wondered why Darcy would wish to stay any longer than necessary at his aunt's house. If Lady Catherine were her aunt, she would find reasons to leave as soon as possible.

She said, "Mr. Darcy strikes me as a man who enjoys doing what he pleases."

The Colonel smiled. "I think we all enjoy that, but as a wealthy man, he has the greater opportunity. More so than those of us who are poor."

She looked at him in polite disbelief – for it was clear that he was in no way poor.

He added, "I speak feelingly. I am a younger son and must practise self-denial."

Elizabeth gave a little laugh. "We must all practise self-denial, sir. No one gets everything they want. And certainly, as the younger son of an Earl, you have more opportunities and choices than most men."

"True," he said. "But my habits of expense make me too dependent. If I wish to free myself, I must marry a woman of fortune."

Elizabeth said, "But at least you have the choice. What is a woman to do? Society does not let us do the proposing."

He looked at her, smiling as if at a secret thought. "I don't think you will have any trouble finding a wealthy man to marry."

Elizabeth said, "Even if I did marry, a woman merely exchanges one master for another – moving from her father's house to her husband's."

"Are you a reader of Mrs. Godwin?"

"I am," she said proudly. She had read *Vindication on the Rights of Woman* and her posthumous works. "I may not agree with all of her actions, but she raised many important questions."

Colonel Fitzwilliam said, "I haven't read her books myself – although one hears about them, of course. Darcy reads them, though. You should talk to him about it."

"I will do that," she said. She would enjoy arguing with him.

They walked to the Parsonage where they could see some workers repairing the roof. The Colonel asked Elizabeth how she had first met his cousin.

"Last autumn," she said. "We met at an assembly, and he was most disagreeable."

The Colonel said, "Please tell me more. I should like to know how he behaves among strangers."

"We were at a ball, and he danced only four dances, even though gentlemen were scarce. Is it any wonder that I found him disagreeable?"

The Colonel smiled. "But you have forgiven him, now, surely."

Elizabeth smiled, not answering. It was difficult to know what she felt about Mr. Darcy. She disliked him, often finding him arrogant and conceited, and yet she was intrigued by him as well. She said, "Tell me what you admire about him."

"He is scrupulously honest."

Elizabeth said, "Which can also be a flaw at times."

"True," the Colonel acknowledged. "Society requires tact and the occasional white lie."

"What else do you admire about him?"

"He is a conscientious landowner. He cares deeply for his sister. He is a good friend."

Elizabeth said, "I have seen that with Mr. Bingley. Mr. Darcy takes a prodigious deal of care of him."

"Ah yes, his friend in Hertfordshire. I think Mr. Bingley is very much indebted to him."

Elizabeth frowned. "Are you saying that Mr. Bingley owes Mr. Darcy money?"

"Oh, no. I meant something else entirely. Darcy said something once, and I assumed he was referring to Bingley."

"What did he say?"

"He said that he had recently saved a friend from a most imprudent marriage. That most likely is Bingley, because Darcy spends so much time with him, and Bingley has a habit of falling in love. He is a romantic."

Elizabeth felt a chill come over her. She said carefully, "Did Mr. Darcy give you his reasons for this interference?"

"I understood that there were some very strong objections against the lady."

Of course, there were, Elizabeth thought, infuriated. Darcy did not want Bingley to marry Jane because of her vulgar uncles. How dare he interfere? How dare he ruin Jane's happiness?

Some of her irritation must have shown on her face, for the Colonel said, "Are you all right?"

Elizabeth made herself smile. "Of course, I am," she prevaricated. "I am merely thinking that Darcy must consider himself a god on Mt. Olympus, interfering with the lives of us mere mortals."

The Colonel laughed. "He is proud, but I don't think he considers himself a god. And he meant to help Bingley. He has a habit of getting into scrapes."

That did not sound good, either. Elizabeth wondered if Jane had had a lucky escape with Bingley leaving Netherfield. She said lightly, "I think we all get into scrapes. That is the weakness of mankind. We do not have crystal balls to see the future."

"I see a Mr. Darcy in your future," the Colonel said wryly.

At first she did not know what he meant, but then Elizabeth looked over to see that Mr. Darcy was approaching them. "That sounds ominous," she teased in a low tone so Darcy could not hear it.

Darcy said, "Ah, Miss Bennet, I am glad I found you. Are you enjoying your walk?"

I was, until you arrived, she thought irritably, but did not say it. She was in no mood to be civil to Mr. Darcy, but she would not cause a scene. She said, "I am, thank you. Rosings has beautiful grounds."

"They are nothing compared to Pemberley, eh Darcy?" the Colonel joked.

Darcy looked uncomfortable with his cousin's banter and said, "I hope someday that you might see Pemberley, Miss Bennet."

Elizabeth said, "Perhaps someday, I will. I know that Miss Bingley spoke very highly of it."

Darcy stared intensely at the Colonel and he said, "Excuse me. I really must be going back to the house. I will leave you two to enjoy the rest of the walk."

Elizabeth said quickly, "No, I have no desire to walk any longer. I will join you."

Darcy said pointedly, "Excuse me, Miss Bennet,

but I would like to speak with you for a moment, if I may."

Elizabeth nodded. "Very well." But if he wanted to speak with her, she would give him a piece of her mind, too. Odious man.

The Colonel left and Elizabeth folded her arms in front of herself, waiting for whatever Mr. Darcy had to say.

He waited until his cousin was too far away to hear them, and then cleared his throat. He said awkwardly, "Miss Bennet, I must speak. I must tell you how ardently I admire and love you."

Elizabeth was astonished. Of all the things he could have said to her, this was the most unexpected.

He continued, "My feelings for you began in Hertfordshire, although initially I fought against them. I knew that my family and friends would not approve of you. But the strength of my feelings could not be denied and now I ask you to make me the happiest man by consenting to become my wife."

Good heavens. Elizabeth knew that although she must refuse him, she should thank him for the honour of his offer, but she was so offended by his arrogance, that she could not form the words. She said instead, "You must be mad."

He looked startled. "I beg your pardon?"

She confronted him. "How could you think that I would ever say yes? That I would accept your proposal? I have never desired your good opinion and you seem to have bestowed it most unwillingly on me. I am sorry to give anyone – including you – pain, but my answer is 'no.'"

Now he looked dumbfounded. His face was pale with anger and he struggled for composure. Eventually, he said stiffly, "And this is all the reply which I am to have the honour of receiving?"

She said, "What else can I say? I have said 'no.' Do you really wish me to explain with all my whys and wherefores?"

"Actually, yes," he said. "For I do not understand it."

"No, I am certain you do not, for it must have never occurred to you that I would say no. You thought your wealth and position would win the day."

He said, "I thought you cared for me. I thought you were expecting my addresses."

"Expecting?" she repeated incredulously. "I

have never heard such conceit. Do you think every woman wants to marry you?"

He said, "But you sought me out."

"When?"

He coloured but his eyes met hers. "When you slept walked. You came to my bedroom."

Elizabeth thought of her dreams. Surely they could not be based on reality. She felt her face colour as well. "When?" she demanded.

"Last night. And also at Netherfield."

Elizabeth did not know what to think. She said hastily, "Even if I did, they were dreams, nothing more."

Darcy reached out to take her hands and she shuddered, stepping back to avoid him. "Don't touch me."

He acted as if she had slapped him. He said, "Forgive me."

She said, "I don't know what I may have done in my sleep to encourage you —"

He looked her directly in the eyes. "You kissed me."

Elizabeth had feared that. She hoped she had done nothing more. She said quickly, "Whatever I have done in my sleep, I must act in my waking hours with integrity."

"I would expect nothing less from you."

She said bluntly, "I don't like you, Mr. Darcy, and I cannot marry you, even if I did kiss you, which I don't remember."

"Do you think I am lying?"

"I don't know what I think. But I know I could never marry a man who separated Mr. Bingley from my sister, thwarting their courtship, ruining my sister's chance at happiness."

"Who told you? Colonel Fitzwilliam?"

"Then you don't deny it?"

"No. Why should I? I did everything in my power to separate my friend from your sister, and indeed, I rejoice in my success. Perhaps towards him I have been kinder than towards myself."

"If that is what you think, you should be relieved that I am refusing you."

Darcy said, "That is not what I meant to say. I am not presenting myself properly. I love you."

"You sound like a petulant child – expecting me to give you what you want merely because you request it. But even if I wished to marry – which I don't – I would never marry a man like you. From the first moment of our meeting, your manners have shown your arrogance, your conceit and your selfish disdain for the feelings of others."

Darcy said, "You don't wish to marry?"

He looked as if he had never imagined a woman saying such a thing.

"No. I consider most marriages to be little better than slavery. I will not be owned. I will not be ruled. So even if you were the ideal man, Mr. Darcy, I would still say no to you."

He said, "You have said quite enough, madam. I perfectly comprehend your feelings and have now only to be ashamed of what my own have been. Forgive me for having demanded your time." He bowed. "Please accept my best wishes for your health and happiness."

And with these words he turned from her and walked away, leaving her to return to Rosings alone.

CHAPTER TWELVE

Darcy waited half an hour before he walked back to Rosings. Colonel Fitzwilliam greeted him as he entered one of the sitting room with, "When is the happy day?"

Fortunately there was no one else present to hear him. Darcy wished he could punch his cousin in the face. "She refused me."

The Colonel was astonished. "But why?"

"Some idiot told her that I kept Bingley from marrying her sister."

The Colonel had the grace to look embarrassed. "I didn't know Bingley wanted to marry Miss Bennet's sister."

"No, and I never told you the specifics. I wish I had never told you anything." He knew that in the future he would be less likely to tell his cousin anything.

"Forgive me, Darcy," the Colonel said. "Is there anything I can do to make amends? Perhaps speak to Miss Bennet?"

"No, I don't want you to say anything to her. Besides, whatever you said was not the entire problem. Apparently she thinks I am arrogant."

The Colonel did not comment. He merely shrugged his shoulders and Darcy said, "Damn you."

The Colonel said, "There is nothing wrong with being arrogant. It suits you."

Darcy smiled despite his high state of frustration. He said finally, "The worst of it is – I feel like a complete fool. I thought she liked me."

Why Elizabeth had sought him out while she was sleepwalking, Darcy would never know, but had he also misread all their conversations? He had thought they were intellectually well-matched.

The Colonel said, "Women are a mystery."

And none more so than Elizabeth Bennet. Darcy said abruptly, "We need to leave tomorrow."

"Are you going to give up the fight?"

"For now," Darcy admitted. He thought it best to live to fight another day. He said, "She is in no mood to listen to me and I must find another way to win her."

THAT EVENING WAS PARTICULARLY AWKWARD for Elizabeth. She said little and refused to look Mr. Darcy in the eyes. Lady Catherine noticed her silence and asked her if she was feeling poorly. Elizabeth confessed that yes, she had a headache, and she was given permission to retire early.

Once in the privacy of her bedroom, she couldn't sleep, and indeed, she was afraid to fall asleep, afraid that she might wander again.

Had she really walked into Mr. Darcy's bedroom?

Whatever must he think of her?

And was that why he had proposed to her?

I must tell you how ardently I admire and love you.

Elizabeth did not think she would ever forget the look on his face when he proposed to her.

And the look on his face when she rejected him.

Part of her was still astonished that he had proposed to her – it was flattering to think that a man of his wealth and position had fallen in love with her. And that he had loved her enough to overcome his disgust for her family and connections.

But she knew if he did marry her, he would come to regret it. Any passion he felt for her would burn out, and like her father, he would find himself unhappily yoked.

And she must never forget what Darcy did to poor Jane.

Odious man.

Elizabeth reminded herself that she did not want to marry anyone.

She then put two chairs in front of her door to keep herself from escaping during the night.

DARCY ROLLED over in his bed and discovered that he was not sleeping alone. Elizabeth Bennet was in his bed, lying beside him, watching him with glassy eyes, and from the way the sheet bared her shoulder, it looked as if she was completely undressed.

Was this a dream?

He reached over to touch her face, caressing her cheek, and she smiled at him, turning her face to kiss his palm.

This was not a dream, but he had seen her so

often in his bedroom that he was becoming accustomed to her visits rather than being startled by them. He supposed it was what their marriage could be like.

He said quietly, "Where is your nightgown?"

She pointed to a chair across the room.

He said, "This isn't proper, and you know it."

She ran her hands over his legs and up under his nightshirt. One hand brushed against his shaft and he groaned. She said, "Do you want me to stay?"

He could not lie and tell her no. Heaven help him; he nodded. She continued her exploration, rubbing her hands on his abdomen. He shuddered and said, "You said you didn't want to marry me. These are not the actions of a woman who wishes to stay single."

She giggled and sat up beside him, kneeling, sitting on her feet. Her breasts were plump, gleaming ivory in the flickering candlelight; her hair fell in curls down past her shoulders to her back. He had never seen a woman so beautiful in his life.

She said, "I won't marry you."

Darcy said calmly. "After tonight, you will have to. Even if you don't like me."

"I don't like you," she said clearly. "But I like this."

Suddenly her hand was wrapped around his cock and blood rushed there so his member strained against her hand.

"Good God," he muttered.

Again she smiled at him. "Now you look like the book. Big and hard. Like a tree branch."

Darcy knew he should pull her hands away from him, but she ran her hand up and down the length of his cock, and he found himself unable to talk.

He reached over to draw her close, to kiss her, but she pressed him back onto the bed so that his back was flat against his mattress. She said, "Hold still."

He gladly obeyed.

He watched her face closely as she climbed up on him, straddling his legs, her breasts swaying slightly. She looked down at him and brushed her hair back over her shoulders, keeping one hand on his cock.

"What are you going to do now?" he asked.

She squeezed him gently and he groaned.

Whatever she did would be fine with him, he decided.

She said, "I know where this goes," and before he could protest, she had raised herself and then impaled herself on his upright member, breathing deep as her tight wet channel gripped him.

Darcy jolted, overcome by the shock and pleasure. "Elizabeth, what have you done?" he gasped.

He never would have taken things this far, but she had been the one to act. He clutched the sheets at his sides, not wanting to alarm her by any sudden movement. "Are you all right?" he asked.

She looked at him thoughtfully. "You are very big." She shifted slightly back and forth, sending ripples of pleasure through him.

"Are you hurt?" From everything he'd heard, he knew that the first time could be difficult for a virgin.

"No," she said calmly. "I am a little uncomfortable but not hurt.

That was good then. He took a deep breath, trying to remain still.

After a moment, she said, "Is this all? From the book, I thought it would be better. This is not as pleasurable as your tongue."

Darcy gave out a little laugh. "That is because you are doing all the work, dearest."

She frowned. "What do you mean?"

"Let me show you." He could not give her back her maidenhead, so he might as well make the loss of it enjoyable.

"Very well."

He carefully lifted her off himself and lay her down beside him, with her head on his pillow. She looked at him trustingly with her wide glassy eyes, and Darcy's heart beat as if it would burst from his chest. He said, "I love you, Elizabeth."

She frowned. "Don't say that."

If she didn't want to hear his declarations, he would show his love by his actions. Darcy took off his nightshirt and tossed it on the floor, which made her smile again. He kissed her lips softly at first, then more urgently. As he kissed her, he massaged her full breasts, playing with her nipples until she gasped and writhed beneath him. She clutched at his shoulders, encouraging him.

Then he reached for her mound, rubbing her through her folds. She sighed and opened her thighs wide for him, granting him access. He kissed her throat and moved his lips down to her breasts as he continued to work between her legs, circling her pearl and pressing his fingers into her tight wet sheath.

"Ah," she breathed out.

He withdrew his fingers and pressed them in again, her liquid making a slick, sucking sound. He continued in a rhythm that made her pant and then moan. "Fitzwilliam!" she gasped.

"What do you want, dearest?"

She groaned. "I want – I want – more."

He used the liquid on his hand to lubricate his aching cock, then pressed his tip against her opening. "I think you are ready now," he said.

"Yes!"

He pressed forward, sinking into her warm quim with one quick thrust. She shuddered and he bit his lip, not wanting to finish before she was satisfied. He lifted himself up, bracing his hands on either side of her so he would not crush her. He moved slowly, pulling himself out a few inches, then thrusting in again, revelling in her slick depths.

Elizabeth wiggled and her thighs tightened on his hips. "Faster," she ordered.

Darcy obeyed. No longer holding himself back, he pushed forward, deeper, harder, pressing Elizabeth against the mattress, making the wooden bed creak.

Elizabeth groaned and writhed, clutching at his arms, then her roving hands moved to his waist and hips; her fingers dug into his buttocks, urging him to take her faster, harder.

He could feel her inner tension as her channel gripped him like a fist, and she arched her hips as if eager to meet every thrust. Then she shuddered, her body convulsing with pleasure.

Darcy, who had been holding himself back, let himself release as well. He groaned as his cock pumped into her, spraying his seed.

For a moment, he could not think, only feel. *La petite mort*, the French called it – the little death.

Darcy felt as if he had died and gone to heaven.

He eased himself down upon her and lay there as his erratic breathing slowed.

Elizabeth rubbed her hands down his back and cupped his buttocks. "Much better," she said with sleepy approval and yawned.

She must marry him now, he thought. But that would be a conversation for the morning. He yawned as well and considered falling asleep beside her. At this moment, he did not care who saw them in the morning. Let Lady Catherine try to separate them; it would not matter. Elizabeth was his and he was hers. He kissed her ear and held her close, nuzzling her neck.

He was half-way asleep, when Elizabeth said, "Fitzwilliam, I must go back to my bedroom."

"Must you?"

She nodded.

Darcy swore and she giggled. Against his better judgment, Darcy found Elizabeth's nightgown on the floor and helped her dress. But first, he took a damp cloth to clean her mound and legs. He used one of his cravats damped by a pitcher of drinking water. What Chetti would think about all of this, he did not know.

Then he escorted her back to her bedroom. "I will talk to you in the morning," he said as he bade her adieu. "And we will settle the matter of marriage once and for all."

CHAPTER THIRTEEN

Elizabeth was in the library at Rosings after break-fast when Darcy found her. She was surprised to see him, for she thought he and Colonel Fitzwilliam planned to leave early in the morning. She saw that Darcy was wearing his travelling coat and Hessian boots.

He said abruptly, "Miss Bennet, Elizabeth, we must speak."

She stiffened. "I have not given you permission to use my name."

"Actually, you have. And you have called me Fitzwilliam."

Elizabeth felt a sense of dread and her eyes widened. She brought one hand up to her throat. "Whatever do you mean?"

"Last night you came to my room again."

"No," she protested. "That can't be true. I – I put chairs in front of my door." Chairs that had been turned over in the morning.

"I know nothing of that. All I know is that last night you were in my bed, naked, and we made love. We must marry."

Elizabeth shuddered. "I don't believe you."

"Did you not feel differently this morning?"

She had felt some discomfort that morning, but nothing out of the ordinary. She felt no differently than if she had taken a strenuous hike. "I remember nothing," she said angrily, "And I will not marry you, even if you did take advantage of me."

He smiled wryly. "Actually, you are the one who took advantage of me. Not that I minded. I love you, Elizabeth, and I think we can be very happy together."

"No," she said. "I do not believe you. I would never – never –." She could not even say the words out loud.

"Seduce me?"

"No."

"Believe me, we did lie together. And you were beneath me, urging me onward."

Over the years, Elizabeth had heard the various

vulgar terms whispered among the servants: Knock. Shag. Tup. Swive. Wap. Making the beast with two backs. She said defiantly, "No. I don't believe you. I think you are saying this to force my hand. To make me marry you."

As soon as she said this, she saw that she had offended him. Darcy drew himself up to his full height and glared at her. "Is that what you think of me? That I would lie about such a matter?"

She lifted her chin defiantly. "Yes, I do."

He looked at her with an expression of mingled incredulity and mortification. She waited, fearing what he would say – what he would do.

But then he bowed. "Then I have nothing else to say to you. Good day, Elizabeth, for after all that we have shared I refuse to call you Miss Bennet."

And then as quickly as he had appeared, he was gone, and Elizabeth sank down upon a chair, exhausted and frightened.

What had she done?

DARCY LEFT for London in a foul mood, refusing to talk to Colonel Fitzwilliam. He had wanted to talk to Elizabeth, to convince her to marry him, but she was so angry, so obstinate, he knew he could not reason with her, and he did not want anyone else to overhear them. So he had retreated.

Whether that was wise, he did not know.

All he knew was that he could not let matters drop between them.

That afternoon, when he was finally settled in Darcy House, he sat at his desk and took out some stationery.

Dear Mr. Bennet, he wrote.

ELIZABETH'S MIND was in a turmoil for the remainder of her visit at Rosings. Whenever she spoke with Charlotte or listened to Lady Catherine gossip about her neighbours, part of her mind kept returning to her last two conversations with Mr. Darcy.

Had she truly gone to his bedroom?

Had she seduced him as he said?

She thought of those pictures in that book and was mortified. In her sleep, had she been no better than a harlot?

She felt as if her world had turned upside down.

She no longer knew herself.

When she left Hunsford, she travelled with Maria to Mr. Gardiner's house in Gracechurch Street, where they stayed for a few days. Then Jane joined them, and the three of them travelled by hired carriage to Hertfordshire where Lydia and Kitty met them at an inn, having come with Mr. Bennet's coachman and his carriage to take them the rest of the way home.

Lydia had ordered a cold luncheon for them but didn't have the money to pay for it, so Jane had to open her reticule. As Kitty and Lydia noisily talked about the news from home, Elizabeth paid little attention.

Lydia said that Wickham was no longer engaged to Miss King and that the militia was going to be encamped near Brighton. "I do so want Papa to take us all there for the summer!" Lydia said. "It would be such a delicious scheme, and I dare say would hardly cost anything at all. Mama would like to go as well. Otherwise, what a miserable summer we shall have without the officers!"

Elizabeth said, "I have had enough of travelling. I wish to stay at home." If sleeping in a new place meant that she slept walked, she never wanted to leave Longbourn again.

Elizabeth wanted to tell Jane about Darcy's

proposal, but the subject was too tender. She did not want Jane to know that Darcy had kept Bingley away from her and she did not want Jane to know that she had gone to Darcy's bedroom several times.

If she had gone.

Elizabeth did not know whether she had gone to his bedroom or not, but despite what she had said, she did not think Mr. Darcy was a liar.

He was arrogant, he was rude, but he was a man who spoke his mind.

For the first few days at home, Lydia and Mrs. Bennet often talked about the possibility of going to Brighton. Mrs. Bennet said that she thought it an excellent idea, but that she would not go sea bathing.

"I want to go sea bathing!" Lydia said and begged their father to take them. "Please! Please! If you take us to Brighton, I shall never ask for anything else ever again."

Elizabeth thought that was unlikely.

And then, when Lydia was beginning to give up hope, the wife of the militia's commander, Mrs. Forster, invited Lydia to come with her to Brighton. Lydia danced about, lording the invitation over her sisters, promising to write and tell them all about her adventures.

Kitty was peevish, saying, "I cannot see why Mrs. Forster should not ask me as well as Lydia, although I am not her particular friend. I have just as much right to be asked as she has, and more, too, for I am two years older."

At this point, Mr. Bennet, who had been listening to their conversation from behind a newspaper, interjected, saying, "Do not pine, Kitty, for even if you were invited, you are not going to Brighton this summer, and neither is your sister Lydia."

Lydia sputtered, "But why not?"

"Because we are all going to Derbyshire."

"Derbyshire?" Mrs. Bennet said. "Why Derbyshire?"

Mr. Bennet looked meaningfully at Elizabeth. "We are all of us going to Pemberley to spend the summer."

Elizabeth's heart sank. She did not want to see Mr. Darcy ever again.

Mrs. Bennet said, "Pemberley? Is that not the home of Mr. Darcy?"

"It is," Mr. Bennet said. "And he wrote to invite us. He also informed me that Mr. Bingley will also be there."

If Darcy had invited Bingley as well as Jane,

that meant that he no longer wished to keep them apart. Elizabeth dreaded seeing Darcy, but she was glad that he was no longer harming Jane's progress.

"Mr. Bingley!" Mrs. Bennet cried, clapping her hands with joy. "Oh, Mr. Bennet, this is the most wonderful news. Brighton is nothing in comparison!"

Lydia would rather go to Brighton with all the officers, but she was mollified by the prospect of a new wardrobe for Mr. Bennet was in a surprisingly generous mood. He told Mrs. Bennet that she could spend what she wished, making certain that all her daughters were well-dressed and looking their best.

"Girls, you have an excellent father," Mrs. Bennet cried. "Haven't I always said so?" She also decided that she liked Mr. Darcy better now. "I did not like him before because I thought he was too formal, but now I see that he can be amiable, as well. He is a handsome man and so tall. I know he doesn't like you, Lizzy, but perhaps he might like one of your sisters. There is no telling what might happen after a month's visit."

At this, Mr. Bennet interrupted to say, "Do not matchmake Mr. Darcy, Mrs. Bennet. He will choose his own wife in his own time." Mr. Bennet looked directly at Elizabeth, who looked down at her lap, disconcerted. What did her father know? What had Mr. Darcy written in his letter?

As they made preparations for the trip, Jane spoke to Elizabeth privately with her concerns. "I have misgivings about this trip."

As do I, Elizabeth thought.

"As much as I look forward to seeing Mr. Bingley again, I wish Mama would not talk so. She thinks that he will propose to me the minute he sees me!"

Elizabeth said, "And if he did – what would you say?"

"Don't tease me, Lizzy," Jane said. "I will admit that I cared for him last year, but now, it is clear that he did not feel the same for me."

"I disagree."

"If he loved me, he would have returned to Netherfield," Jane said simply. "I pray that when we meet again, it can be without embarrassment – like common and indifferent acquaintances, but that will be impossible if Mama keeps fussing about us."

Elizabeth did not know what to say to her. She knew that Darcy had kept them apart before, but now, he had made a point of inviting Bingley when they were to visit, which implied that he had changed his mind.

"There is nothing we can do about Mama. If we try to quiet her, she will only be more determined. So, I think it is best to guard your heart," Elizabeth advised. "And observe how Mr. Bingley behaves. Within a day or so, you will know if he loves you."

Jane said, "Even if he does love me, that does not mean that he will propose."

Elizabeth acknowledged the truth of her words. She thought of Mr. Darcy's proposals – both of them – and how she had angrily refused him. Was his invitation his way to propose again? She said, "All we can do is to wait and see."

Jane nodded and sighed. "You are right."

As the days passed, Elizabeth grew concerned about another matter. Normally, she and her sisters had their menses simultaneously, usually starting within a week of each other, but as May ended, she had not started to bleed.

Every day in early June, Elizabeth waited and wondered.

By the time they left for Pemberley, she knew that she was pregnant.

She knew now that Darcy had told her the truth, that somehow, she had gone to his bedroom in the middle of the night and they had made love.

She was horrified. She knew what happened to young women who gave birth without being married.

She and her family would be ruined.

Her father, noticing that she was not her usual happy self, said, "You seem to be rather pensive, Lizzy. Do you have something to tell me?"

Elizabeth shook her head. "No, sir." She must talk to Mr. Darcy before she spoke to her father.

CHAPTER FOURTEEN

ELIZABETH, as they drove along, watched for the first appearance of Pemberley Woods with some perturbation; and when at length they turned in at the lodge, her spirits were in a high flutter.

The park was very large and contained great variety of ground. They entered it in one of its lowest points and drove for some time through a beautiful wood which stretched over a wide extent. Mr. Bennet commented, "I think you shall enjoy walking here, Lizzy."

Elizabeth's mind was too full for conversation, but she saw and admired the property. Of all this, she could have been mistress.

Mrs. Bennet gasped as they left the woods and suddenly Pemberley House was before them on the opposite side of a valley. Pemberley was a large, handsome, stone building standing well on rising ground, backed by a ridge of high woody hills and in front, a stream had been swelled into a glistening pond. "What a magnificent home," Mrs. Bennet declared. "I don't care which of you marries Mr. Darcy, but one of you should."

Mary said, "One should not marry a man merely for a house."

No, Elizabeth thought, but it was a beautiful house, nonetheless.

"Thank you, Mary," Mr. Bennet said dryly.

"It is more than the house," Mrs. Bennet reminded. "Mr. Darcy has ten thousand pounds a year, if not more. Anyone who marries him will have carriages, jewels and I can't even imagine the pin money."

Mr. Bennet said, "That is enough, madam."

Mrs. Bennet pursed her lips, somewhat chastened.

"And please, everyone, try not to be so silly when we meet the man himself. If you cannot speak in a rational manner, be silent."

Mrs. Bennet said, "I believe all of us will be on our best behaviour, sir."

He continued. "And I hope that none of you are

so mercenary that you would marry a man you do not like and admire."

Elizabeth could not help but wonder if her mother had married her father for his home – Longbourn.

Mr. Bennet added humorously, "But to be fair, I have heard it said that it is as easy to fall in love with a rich man as a poor man."

"If not easier," Mrs. Bennet murmured rebelliously.

They were met at the door by a housekeeper, Mrs. Reynolds. She was a respectable-looking, elderly woman, much less fine and more civil than Elizabeth had expected. She showed them to a large sitting room and asked if they would like refreshment after their travel. Liveried servants were sent outside to gather their trunks and take them upstairs to their bedrooms. Elizabeth noticed that the rooms were lofty and tastefully decorated. There was nothing gaudy or uselessly fine. Everything about Pemberley appeared proper and elegant.

"The master will be here at any moment," Mrs. Reynolds said.

Elizabeth steeled herself, not knowing what to think and how to feel.

And then sooner than she expected, he was before her, walking into the drawing room with a young woman behind him, presumably his younger sister Georgiana.

Darcy was just as she remembered – tall and handsome, but with a look on his face that she had never seen before. He greeted her parents with more than civility – he was warm and accommodating, asking about their travel and assuring them that every effort would be made for their comfort.

She had never seen him so polite and well-behaved.

He introduced them to his sister, Georgiana. She was a tall young woman, handsome in her way, and very shy. Her manners were perfectly unassuming and gentle. Mr. Darcy mentioned that his sister enjoyed playing the pianoforte and suggested that she might enjoy practising with Miss Mary or Miss Elizabeth.

Georgiana smiled at Elizabeth. "I would like that."

They were also joined by Mr. Bingley, without his sisters fortunately, for they had chosen to remain in Town. Elizabeth thought it likely that they had declined an invitation when they knew that the Bennets would be coming as well.

Elizabeth watched how Bingley could not keep from smiling at her sister and she thought it likely that all of Jane's fears were unfounded. She had never seen a man so in love.

Elizabeth glanced at Darcy, wondering what he was thinking.

DARCY WENT through the motions of meeting Elizabeth's family, but he stole every possible look at her. Elizabeth was even more beautiful than he had remembered.

She was thinner than he remembered, and pale, and he hoped that she was not ill.

She looked at him warily, though, and he wished he could whisk her away to talk to her privately, but instead, he must be a polite host. But somehow, he would find a way to meet with her – and not before she wandered out of her bed at night.

As much as he craved another nocturnal visit with her, he had arranged for a servant to sit outside her door at night so she could not leave her bedroom.

He offered to give them a tour of his house. Mr.

Bennet declined. "Just show me to your library, sir, and I will be content."

"As you wish."

Mrs. Bennet said she needed to rest before dinner, and the younger girls were more interested in the grounds. Mr. Bingley offered to take them all for a walk outdoors. "I think you will like it very much," he said. "And we have a choice. The shorter walk is two miles, but there is a longer route that is ten miles in circumference."

Elizabeth acted as if she would join them, but Darcy whispered to her, "Let me show you my house."

There was a flash of fear in her eyes as she looked at him, which made his heart ache, but then she said, "Very well, sir. Thank you." At first, Georgiana accompanied them, but at his prompting, she excused herself to fetch a shawl.

Finally, he and Elizabeth were alone.

They were in the picture gallery, where there were numerous paintings of his ancestors. As much as he wished to introduce his family to Elizabeth, he wanted more to speak to her. He said, "Miss Bennet, Elizabeth," at the same time that she said, "Mr. Darcy."

He waited for her to finish.

She took a deep breath and said quickly, "I must speak, even though you may regret what I have to say. First, I apologize for not believing you when we last spoke at Rosings."

"You have remembered?"

"No," she said flatly. "I am with child."

Darcy's thoughts raced. A child? He and Elizabeth were having a child? He was overcome by a wave of happiness that filled his chest. "That is wonderful. I mean, are you well? How are you feeling?"

"I am slightly ill in the mornings, but other than that, I am fine."

"Excellent," he said. "I will speak to your father and arrange for the minister. I have already arranged for a special license. I hope you don't think that was presumptuous of me."

"It was presumptuous," she said. "Because I still don't wish to marry you."

He felt stunned. "I don't understand."

"I don't wish to marry anyone."

"Because?"

"Because men rule the world, but they will not rule me."

His cousin had mentioned that Elizabeth had radical thoughts about women and their place in society. He said, "So you want our child to be a bastard."

"No," she said quickly.

"That is what will happen if you don't marry me."

She clutched her hands before her. "I hoped that we could think of another solution."

The distress on her face touched his heart. He said rashly, "I will do whatever I can to make you happy. If you want to go somewhere and give birth to this baby, without marrying me, you can do it. I will raise the child as my own."

"I will not abandon my child."

"This is my child as well."

She said, "I have heard rumours that the Duchess of Devonshire had a child that was not her husband's."

"Yes, but she was not allowed to keep it. If you want to keep our baby, you must marry me."

Elizabeth's eyes filled with tears and he wanted to comfort her, but that was not his place. Not yet. She said finally, "If I marry you, I want us to be friends. I want to have a marriage of equals."

"I don't think that is possible. No two people are equal."

"Not in everything, I agree," she said. "Ideally,

each partner has their strengths and weaknesses that counterbalance each other. But I am thinking of equality – as two men friends are equal. Like you and Mr. Bingley. I don't want you to tell me what to do. To make my decisions for me."

It was a new concept for Darcy, but he was willing to take a chance on such a relationship if it meant that he could have Elizabeth. He said, "I don't know how such a marriage would proceed, but I am willing to try."

"And if I don't like being married to you, I want us to live apart."

Darcy did not like that idea. He said, "Pemberley is large enough that you would not have to see me except at the dinner table, if you wished."

She nodded. "All right."

"Do you have any other demands?"

She coloured. "I don't – I don't want to do the thing that would create a child."

He smiled at her discomfort. "It is too late for that."

"I meant in the future. I don't want other children."

Darcy definitely did not like this idea, either. "You wish to be celibate?"

She lifted her chin. "Yes."

Was she testing him? He said, "Why? Have you remembered our time together? Did you not enjoy yourself?" Had he shocked her or given her a disgust of him?

She said, "No, I don't remember any of it. I don't know why God in His wisdom requires such actions to create a child. But it seems so uncomfortable, awkward, and embarrassing."

Darcy knew he shouldn't laugh, but he was amused by her concerns. He smiled and said gently, "I agree. With the wrong person, it is disagreeable. But with you, it is glorious."

She looked at him, surprised. "It is?"

How he loved her. "Yes."

She said, "I wish I could remember more."

So did he. It was difficult to remember that she was a gently bred young woman and no longer the virago she was when she walked in her sleep. That woman would have kissed him by now, but this woman he must woo carefully. He said, "What exactly have you been told about the process?"

"I don't know all the particulars, but I have seen animals in the barn, and there was a book, you see."

Darcy removed a small book from his coat pocket. "This one?"

"Good heavens," she said, her eyes widening. "Was it your book all along?"

"Yes. Do you want to look at it again?" He flipped through the pages so she could see some of the illustrations.

She shook her head, shuddering. She held up her hands as if to protect herself. "No, but if you own it, you must understand why I wouldn't want to do any of that. It is so –," she searched for the right word, "wicked."

He leaned forward and brushed his hand across her cheek. "It is not wicked when two people love each other."

She hesitated but did not pull away. "I don't love you," she said bravely.

Darcy knew that Elizabeth would never tell him what he wanted to hear; she would always tell him the truth and he respected that. "I know. But I think in time, you may change your mind and come to love me as much as I love you."

She nodded, still wary, but listening to him. "All right then."

The words thrilled him. He touched his fingertip to her lips and said, "Besides, I think I know you better than you know yourself. It is said *in vino veritas.* I think for us, we can say *in somniorum non est verum.*"

She said, "In dreams there is truth?"

"Precisely." He continued to rub his finger softly across her lips, making her sigh. "You said something about it before. That Queen Mab gives us in dreams what we inwardly desire."

Elizabeth frowned slightly. "I had forgotten that."

"Then let me kiss you," he urged. "Let me remind you."

CHAPTER FIFTEEN

DARCY WANTED TO KISS HER.

Elizabeth felt as if her heart was beating so loudly that he would be able to hear it. She knew she shouldn't be missish. He had kissed her before. They had done things – things to create a child – but she could not remember any of it.

And now he wanted to kiss her.

She nodded, intrigued, but still feeling shy, unable to speak.

He placed one hand under her chin and tilted her face upward and bent downward so his lips could reach hers.

He was so tall that perhaps they would need a step stool, she thought, amused, but then his lips were on hers – so gently with the faintest touch.

She closed her eyes, wanting to feel every sensation.

He kissed her again, this time, sucking her bottom lip into his mouth and nibbling on it.

She gasped, eyes opening.

"Do you not like that?" he asked as he kissed her again.

"I don't know."

He said, "You can stop me at any time, darling."

Darling. As much as Elizabeth did not know what she felt for him, he seemed to care for her. She relaxed, letting him kiss her.

She decided that she liked his mouth on hers, even when his tongue rubbed against hers. All his motions were soft and slow, careful, as if he didn't want to frighten her.

He kissed her again and again, now trailing his lips across her throat to her ear. She liked this as well. He said quietly, "You can touch me."

She realized that her hands were in tight fists against his chest. She released her tight grip and placed her hands flat, pressing them gingerly on the fabric of his waistcoat, directly over his broad chest. He murmured, "much better," and wrapped one arm around her waist, drawing her closer as he continued to kiss her.

As they snuggled together, one of his hands brushed against her bosom. The point of her breast throbbed. Elizabeth pulled back, confused by the jolt of pleasure his touch gave her.

"What is it?" he asked.

She was so embarrassed; she could not look him in the eyes. "My breasts," she murmured.

"Did I hurt you?"

She shook her head, completely mortified.

He looked at her closely, trying to read her expression. "Ah," he said finally. "Did you like that?"

She nodded.

He let out his breath with a little puff of air and smiled at her. "Let me help you," he said, sounding slightly amused, and then calmly unbuttoned her spencer. He palmed one breast, over her dress, which felt so good that she said, "oh,' and smiled at him.

He addressed each of her breasts, rubbing and caressing them over her clothes. When he pinched at her cloth covered nipples, she groaned.

At this, he slid one hand into the neckline of her

dress, but as his fingers cupped her warm flesh, she gasped and pulled back. "Mr. Darcy!"

He read the alarm and censure in her tone and retreated, removing his hand. "Forgive me, Elizabeth," he said as he carefully smoothed her lace fichu. "I will remember that I am a gentleman and not disrobe you before we are married."

Elizabeth was horrified by what she had allowed and how good it felt. But she maintained her sense of humour and said, "I realize that it is a little like shutting the barn door after a steed has been stolen, but I do appreciate your restraint. Thank you."

Darcy looked at her closely. "I only want to please you, Elizabeth – now and when we are married."

He seemed sincere and his words reassured her. Perhaps marriage to him would not be the ordeal she had imagined. She sighed. "Very well. You may speak to my father and set a date. Although I dread what he will think of me."

Darcy said, "Do not concern yourself. He already knows that we anticipated our vows."

"What? You told him?" Elizabeth was appalled, but that explained the looks her father had given her.

"I wrote to him. That is why you were all invited to Pemberley. I planned to propose again and get married as soon as possible, but we will act even more quickly now that I know you are expecting."

Elizabeth felt like a fox being treed by hounds. Any sense of choice she had felt earlier was illusionary. Darcy and her father would see that she was wed. "How soon do you wish to do this?"

"Within the next two weeks," he answered. "I would like to invite my uncle, the Earl of Matlock and several of my cousins. And you may invite Mr. and Mrs. Gardiner and the Philips's."

Elizabeth nodded, grateful that he was willing to open his house to her relations who were in Trade. "Thank you."

He held out the small book. "And until then, perhaps you would like to read this more closely. To prepare yourself for marriage."

Elizabeth hesitated. She wanted to look at the book, although she knew it was not proper. Her parents, everyone she knew, would be scandalized by it.

He said gently, "There should be no secrets between a husband and wife."

Elizabeth looked up at him. "You don't think poorly of me?"

He gave a little laugh. "No, indeed. In truth, I feel as I have been given a gift. I cannot imagine anyone that I would like to marry more than you."

"Thank you." Elizabeth took the book and slipped it into the pocket of her dress.

Before dinner, Darcy spoke to her father and then Mr. Bennet spoke to Elizabeth privately in one of Pemberley's sitting rooms. "I did not want to discuss the matter until it was resolved," Mr. Bennet said, "But I trust that you are willing to marry him?"

Elizabeth wondered what he would say if she said 'no.' She said, "Yes, I am willing."

Mr. Bennet nodded. "I know Mr. Darcy is not the sort of man either of us expected for you, but he seems to be a man of honour, and I appreciate that. He also seems to be a man of sense. He is well-read and I hope that the two of you will find a way to get along somehow. And if not, at least he owns several properties, so you needn't live together."

His hope for her future seemed a bleak one, and Elizabeth sensed that her father wished that he could live separately from her mother. "Thank you, sir."

"Oh, and don't tell your mother about the

baby," Mr. Bennet recommended. "She cannot keep a secret and it is best if no one knows. You won't be the first woman to give birth to an early child, and as long as Mr. Darcy doesn't mind, it won't matter."

"Yes, sir."

At dinner, Darcy rose to his feet and gave a toast – to Elizabeth. "I give you Miss Elizabeth Bennet, soon to be Elizabeth Darcy." Everyone was startled by his announcement, but Mrs. Bennet was the most surprised. "You want to marry Lizzy? But I thought she was not handsome enough to dance with!"

Darcy had the grace to look uncomfortable for a moment, but he added quickly, "I hope Elizabeth and everyone else will kindly forget that I ever made such a foolish comment. Rest assured, Mrs. Bennet, I now find your second daughter to be most beauti-ful." He raised his glass. "Miss Elizabeth Bennet."

After everyone drank in Elizabeth's honour, Bingley said he wished to make a toast as well. He stood and announced, "To Miss Jane Bennet, soon to be Jane Bingley."

At this, Jane blushed happily, and Mrs. Bennet looked as if she might swoon. "Mr. Bingley, are you joking?"

"No, ma'am," he said solemnly.

Mr. Bennet interjected that Bingley had already spoken with him. "I am sad to lose both of my eldest daughters, but I hope they will be very happy." He smiled at them all.

Mrs. Bennet said, "Oh, my dear, dear Jane. I knew how it would be. I was sure you could not be so beautiful for nothing! And dear, dear Lizzy. How wise you were not to accept Mr. Collins. Mr. Darcy will be hundred times a better husband."

Elizabeth said wryly, "I think so." She glanced briefly at Darcy to see what he thought of her mother's comments. He did not roll his eyes, but she knew he was tempted.

Mrs. Bennet continued. "I am so happy. To think that I will have two daughters married." She clutched her hands over her heart. "I don't know if I can bear such happiness. I have such flutterings in my chest."

"Please, Mama," Elizabeth said. "Why don't you drink more of Mr. Darcy's excellent wine."

"Or lie down," Jane suggested.

"No, I shall rally," Mrs. Bennet assured them. "This is the best day of my life."

The rest of the evening was spent talking about wedding plans. Darcy assured Mrs. Bennet that she could invite any of her friends and that he would provide an excellent wedding breakfast at Pemberley.

Mrs. Bennet was concerned when learning that the weddings were to be held in two weeks, for that was insufficient time to obtain all the weddings clothes, but she was relieved that all of her daughters had new gowns. "I am beginning to think that you knew some of this, Mr. Bennet," she teased him.

"I had an inkling," he admitted.

That evening, when she prepared for bed, Elizabeth was informed that a maid servant would sit outside her door in the hallway. "All night?" she asked.

"Yes, ma'am," the lady's maid informed her. "She slept earlier so she can remain awake all night."

Elizabeth supposed it was for the best. No doubt Darcy did not want her to wander about Pemberley.

Jane crept from her bedroom to Elizabeth's so they could also talk that evening. Elizabeth hugged Jane and congratulated her on becoming engaged to marry Bingley. "How marvellous that he did love you, after all."

Jane blushed. "I am so happy. I do not deserve it."

"Nonsense. If anyone deserves happiness, you do."

Jane said, "And I am even more happy to think that you will marry his good friend. We may live apart, but we will be able to visit each other often."

Elizabeth nodded. "I shall insist upon it."

Jane hesitated. "But dear sister, I am a trifle concerned. For a long time you seemed to dislike Mr. Darcy, and now you are engaged to him. At dinner, I was as astonished as our mother. What made you change your mind?"

Elizabeth thought of the infant growing in her womb. She said, "I believe my change of heart has been coming on gradually. And I wish I had not been so vehement in my dislike before. I thought I was so clever, finding his flaws and joking about them. But you must forget all that now."

"I will," Jane promised. "I just want to make certain you are not marrying him without affection."

Elizabeth hoped she would not be damned for lying. She said, "I care for him well enough. And now, having seen Pemberley and its beautiful grounds, I like him even more."

Jane laughed. "Now I know you are teasing me. Please be serious."

Elizabeth said, "I am. I am. You know how much I like trees and rocks and Mr. Darcy has an abundance of both."

"Lizzy," Jane entreated.

"And he kisses very well."

Jane gasped. "You have kissed Mr. Darcy?"

Elizabeth did not know how to answer that, so she took a defensive stance. "Haven't you kissed Mr. Bingley?"

"Not on the lips," Jane said in horrified tones. "He kissed my hand, but everything else will wait until we are married."

"That is best," Elizabeth agreed. She had a feeling that she would not be lending her little book to Jane or Bingley.

CHAPTER SIXTEEN

THE NEXT FEW days were busy with preparations for the wedding. Mrs. Reynolds, the housekeeper, spoke with Elizabeth about the wedding breakfast. Elizabeth felt some awkwardness at first, but she knew that as the future Mistress of Pemberley, she must become accustomed to directing the various servants.

Mrs. Reynolds was a kindly, amiable woman, and she was thrilled by the engagement. "Everyone at Pemberley is pleased. I have hoped for a long time that the Master would find a bride, but I wasn't certain he could find a young woman good enough for him."

Elizabeth smiled, thinking that her statement could be taken in two ways – either Darcy was such a paragon that no woman would be worthy of him, or he was so arrogant and exacting that he would not think any young woman up to his standards. She said, "I hope I will do him proud."

Mrs. Reynolds continued, "Oh, to be sure, I know you will."

As they planned menus and talked about decorations and sleeping arrangements for the guests, Mrs. Reynolds sprinkled their conversation with additional praise of Mr. Darcy. She said that he was the best landlord and the best master that ever lived. "He has never been wild, like so many young men now-a-days, who think of nothing but themselves. There is not one of his tenants or servants but what will give him a good name. Some people call him proud; but I am sure I never say anything of it. To my fancy, it is only because he does not rattle away like other young men."

This was an interesting perspective. Elizabeth assumed that instead of proud, Darcy could be considered reticent. In public, he chose his words carefully. That was a quality she could admire, particularly after living with her mother.

Mrs. Reynolds also said that she had never had a cross from Mr. Darcy in her life, and she had known him since he was four years old.

Elizabeth did not believe her, but said politely, "There are very few people of whom so much can be said."

"It is all true," Mrs. Reynolds continued. "I don't think I have ever met a better man. But I have always observed, that they who are good-natured when children, are good-natured when they grow up; and he was always the sweetest tempered, most generous-hearted boy in the world."

Later, when Elizabeth spoke to Darcy privately in the library, she teased him that Mrs. Reynold thought he had been a perfect child and now was a perfect man. He demurred, shaking his head. "I will not accuse her of senility, but she is too kind in her memory. I tried to be an obedient child, and I was taught what was right by my excellent parents. But I was not taught to correct my temper. I was given good principles, but I was left to follow them in pride and conceit. For many years I was an only child, and my parents let me be selfish and over-bearing."

"You begin to frighten me," Elizabeth said archly.

"No, I hope not," he said quickly as he took her hands in his. "I have been a selfish being all my life, but meeting you, falling in love with you has changed me, making me want to be a better person. When you refused to marry me, I was properly humbled. I come before you now, eager to prove myself."

At this, he kissed her hands and Elizabeth did not pull away.

She thought that neither of them were without flaws, and if they worked together, perhaps they could make a happy marriage. After he kissed her hands, he looked up at her and smiled.

Since her first day at Pemberley, he had been very circumspect, never kissing her on the lips, never taking any physical liberties. Elizabeth knew Darcy was waiting until they were married, but sometimes she wished he would throw caution to the wind and pull her against him and crush her lips under his.

Perhaps this was due to his book that she was looking at late at night. She looked at the pictures by candlelight and hid the book under her mattress in the mornings.

"Are you all right?" Darcy asked. "You look a little pale."

"I am fine," she assured him.

Mrs. Reynolds was not the only person who sang Mr. Darcy's praises. His sister Georgiana also told Elizabeth that he was an ideal brother. "He and my cousin Colonel Fitzwilliam are my guardians and they have taken excellent care of me."

"I am glad to hear it," Elizabeth said. "And I envy you, a little. I always wanted a brother."

Georgiana said, "And I always wanted a sister."

Elizabeth liked Georgiana and felt that in time, she would truly be a sister to her. They spoke of books and music, and Elizabeth asked her if she wanted to go to London for the season.

Georgiana said that she was not ready for such a step.

Elizabeth was surprised, and Georgiana explained. "Last year, I fell in love."

"Oh no," Elizabeth breathed out. "What happened? Did your brother interfere?"

Georgiana nodded. "But he was right to do so. The man I loved was not a good man. He had been my friend when we were younger, but then he kissed me and wanted me to elope with him."

Thanks to Darcy, Elizabeth knew how persuasive kisses could be. Elizabeth nodded, encouraging her future sister-in-law to continue.

Georgiana said, "I knew it was wrong, but I

agreed. And I would have run off with him if my brother hadn't come to visit me. I was in Ramsgate with one of my teachers. When I told Fitzwilliam about Mr. Wickham —"

"Wickham?" Elizabeth interrupted. "George Wickham?"

"Yes. Do you know him?"

"I did. Briefly. My sister Lydia is more of his friend. He is a soldier in the local militia. They were stationed by our home in Hertfordshire, but now he is in Brighton."

"She should be careful. He is not to be trusted. He is a fortune hunter."

Elizabeth was reminded of his engagement to Miss King. She said, "My sister Lydia does not have a large fortune. Her dowry is quite small."

"Then he won't marry her," Georgiana said flatly. "He would only break her heart. He only wanted me because my dowry is thirty thousand pounds."

Elizabeth was impressed with the sum, but said kindly, "I doubt that. Any man would be fortunate to marry you even without a dowry."

"No, it is true," Georgiana said. "He admitted as much. Darcy sent him away and brought me back to Pemberley to live at home."

"Was he very angry?"

"Only at Wickham; never at me. He was very kind and did not blame me at all. In truth, he blamed himself, saying that he should have taken greater care in choosing my chaperone – and that he should have visited me more often." Georgiana smiled. "As much as I regret the past, I feel that it has brought us closer as brother and sister."

"You are very fortunate, then."

"I am," Georgiana agreed.

Elizabeth had noticed that Darcy treated his sister with kindness, attending to her needs and encouraging her. She'd heard from Mrs. Reynolds that he had just bought Georgiana a new pianoforte. As the housekeeper said, "Whatever can give his sister any pleasure is sure to be done in a moment. There is nothing he would not do for her."

Elizabeth added, "I hope your heart is fully recovered."

Georgiana sighed. "I don't know if I will ever fall in love again. I don't know if I could ever trust a man."

"I understand," Elizabeth said with empathy. "Marriage can be a frightening prospect."

Georgiana smiled. "But not for you, surely."

Elizabeth did not want to malign her future husband. "No, of course not," she said lightly. "I spoke in generalities. A woman must be very careful to choose a man who will take good care of her and not mistreat her."

"You won't find a better man than my brother," Georgiana assured her.

"No, I think not," Elizabeth agreed. The more she learned about him, the more she approved of him.

"And he adores you."

Elizabeth was flustered. "He said so?"

"He doesn't need to tell me. I can see it on his face when you walk into a room. And your liveliness has softened him. He is not so formal. He laughs more."

Elizabeth said, "That is good. I do love to laugh." She thought her married life would be very dull if she could not laugh.

Georgiana said, "I think you will be very happy together."

OVER THE NEXT FEW DAYS, Elizabeth watched how Darcy spent time with her father, talking to him about various books and farming methods, and playing chess with him in the evenings. Darcy also spoke to her mother, promising her that the three younger girls could have a season in London the next spring, if they wished.

When Lydia and Kitty heard this, they squealed and danced around, which made Darcy wince and Elizabeth laugh.

She did ask him, privately, however, how she could assist with her sisters' season if she had a new baby.

Darcy placed a discrete hand on her stomach and told her not to worry. "I will ask my aunt Lady Matlock to manage it. She recently found a husband for her last daughter and she will enjoy the challenge of finding husbands for your sisters."

"Even Lydia?"

Darcy frowned. "Perhaps not Lydia. She is still rather young to be much in company."

Elizabeth agreed, although she did not think her mother would restrain her. Elizabeth debated whether she should tell him that Lydia had thought she was in love with Wickham, but then she decided to tell him later. Wickham was in another county and should not cause any further trouble.

"You are very generous," she told him. "And if

you are not careful, my parents will consider you their favourite son-in-law and never leave Pemberley. Mr. Bingley and Netherfield Park will be nothing in comparison."

"No, I am not worried. I think your father wants to return to his library, and your mother wants to return to Longbourn so she can tell all her friends in Meryton about us."

Elizabeth thought he might be right.

When the Gardiners and the Philips's arrived, Darcy spoke with them as well, being a gracious host.

Mrs. Gardiner said to Elizabeth, "I like your Mr. Darcy very well. His father was an excellent man, and it appears that his son will follow in his footsteps." Mrs. Gardiner had spent much of her youth in Lambton, a small town by Pemberley, so she and Mr. Darcy had some acquaintances in common.

Darcy also invited Mr. Gardiner to go fishing, which pleased her uncle. He told her later, "I thought that with his wealth and position, he might be a proud man, but instead, he is perfectly well behaved, polite and unassuming."

From what Elizabeth could see, nearly everyone

liked Mr. Darcy, and with their approbation, her concerns about her future life lessened.

She even liked his grand relatives – the Earl of Matlock and Lady Matlock who arrived with Colonel Fitzwilliam a day before the wedding. The Earl was a large, jovial man who reminded her of Sir William Lucas, and Lady Matlock was a very tall, thin woman, beautifully dressed, who talked about all her friends in London.

The Matlocks were happy to welcome her into their family, and although not thrilled with her relatives, they were civil.

When Colonel Fitzwilliam saw Elizabeth, he teased, "I remember telling you once that Mr. Darcy would be in your future. And I was right."

She smiled. "You were clairvoyant, sir."

That evening, before dinner, Darcy asked Elizabeth to meet him in the library, where they could talk privately. Elizabeth slipped away from her family and joined him. Once the library door was closed, he pulled her close and kissed her briefly. He said, "Tomorrow we will be man and wife."

The prospect no longer frightened her. Elizabeth looked up at him and sighed happily. "I have one additional request."

He said, "As much as I would like to say, 'anything for you,' I am not so rash."

"That is wise," she said. "My request is more of a question. Do you mind or will you mind what clothes I wear?"

He frowned. "I don't understand."

Elizabeth said, "The fashions for women are restrictive. I cannot raise my arms all the way over my head without ripping the seams." She motioned, showing him her restraints.

"Good heavens," he said. "That is ridiculous."

"I agree," she said. "But it is fashionable. So, my question for you is whether I can dress as I please, or if I must be fashionable as your Mrs. Darcy."

"You can wear whatever you like. As long as you do not traipse around in public half naked like Venus, I will not complain."

At that moment, Elizabeth realized that she might be falling in love with him after all. She smiled. "No, I shall only do that in private," she teased.

He looked stunned. "Truly? I thought you would be too shy for that."

She felt herself blush. "Your little book is helping me overcome my shyness."

"Excellent," he said and kissed her again. But

when she reached up to link her hands behind his neck, he demurred. He separated her hands and brought them before him. He kissed them, instead of her lips, and said, "As much as I would like to ignore our guests, forget dinner, and spend the rest of the day kissing you, I cannot. But I promise, tomorrow, as soon as the wedding breakfast is over, we will leave everyone behind."

Elizabeth knew that the plan was for them to honeymoon in London at Darcy House. She said, "I will like that."

CHAPTER SEVENTEEN

DARCY STOOD beside Elizabeth in the chapel at Lambton, just as Bingley stood beside Jane. The minister began the familiar words: *Dearly beloved, we are gathered together here in the sight of God, and in the face of this congregation to join together this Man and this Woman in holy matrimony; which is an honourable estate.*

As the man spoke, Darcy glanced at Elizabeth, thinking that she was the most beautiful bride and he was the most fortunate man in England.

When the minister said that marriage was ordained for the procreation of children, he thought of the child Elizabeth carried.

Marriage was also ordained for the mutual society, help, and comfort that the one ought to have of the other.

Please God, Darcy prayed silently. *Help me to be an excellent husband.*

When the minister said, "If any man can shew any just cause, why they may not lawfully be joined together, let him now speak," Darcy held his breath. He had heard tales of weddings being interrupted, even though he had never seen it.

Just then a strident female voice said, "Stop this wedding this instant!"

Darcy turned to see his aunt Lady Catherine de Bourgh striding into the church, dragging her daughter Anne behind her. Lady Catherine repeated, "Stop this wedding immediately."

"Catherine!" the Earl of Matlock said. "What are you doing?"

Lady Catherine glared at him. "My lord, I can't believe you are a party to this travesty."

At this point, the minister cleared his throat. "Pardon me, madam. Who are you and what is your objection?"

Lady Catherine pulled herself up to her full height and said haughtily. "I am Lady Catherine de Bourgh. This man-" she pointed to Darcy, "is my nephew and he is engaged to my daughter, Anne. So he cannot marry this –" she pointed at Elizabeth "upstart."

The minister said to Darcy, "Is there any truth to this assertion?"

"No, none," Darcy said firmly.

Lady Catherine said, "Their engagement was of a peculiar kind. From their infancy, they have been intended for each other. It was the favourite wish of his mother, as well as of hers. While in their cradles, we planned the union."

Darcy took Elizabeth's hand in his and squeezed it to encourage her. He said loudly, "Regardless of the wishes of my mother, I have never been engaged to my cousin Anne de Bourgh."

The minister said, "Miss de Bourgh, are you engaged to Mr. Darcy?"

"No, sir," she said in a weak voice.

"Did he ever make any promises of marriage to you?"

"No, sir."

Lady Catherine said, "But that is not true. You both know you were made for each other! Whom will you marry if not your cousin?"

"She will marry me."

Darcy looked and saw his cousin Colonel Fitzwilliam standing. He added, "Miss de Bourgh is engaged to me."

Lady Catherine swayed on her feet, as if she might faint. "That is impossible."

The minister asked, "And you are?"

"Richard Fitzwilliam."

"My son. My second eldest," the Earl interjected.

"Is this true?" the minister asked Anne.

Anne considered their cousin for a moment, then said loudly, "Yes, it is true."

The Colonel flashed her a brilliant smile.

"Anne, what have you done?" Lady Catherine demanded as she tugged on her arm. "Let us go home. I refuse to acknowledge this engagement, if it even exists, which I doubt."

Anne stood her ground, refusing to move. "I want to stay for the wedding."

Darcy thought this might very well be the first time she had refused to obey her mother.

The Colonel moved to stand beside her as if wishing to strengthen her resolve.

Lady Catherine glared at them. "I am most seriously displeased."

The Earl bristled. "Catherine, do you object to my son?" he demanded. "If you were willing to marry her to one cousin, there should be no objection to another."

"But he has no property!" Lady Catherine argued.

"And neither did you when you married Sir Lewis," the Earl reminded. "But Anne will inherit Rosings, which should be sufficient for them both."

"Then you approve of this arrangement?"

"I do," the Earl said. "And I will do everything in my power to facilitate it."

Lady Catherine looked between her daughter and her brother, dumbfounded and angry at her inability to get her way. "This is not right," she muttered. "But I see that I am overruled."

The minister smiled to smooth the matter. "And now, if you please, let us finish with the weddings at hand. The rest of the matters you may resolve among yourselves at a later time."

Darcy squeezed Elizabeth's hand and she responded with a similar squeeze.

The ceremony continued, and when at last they were pronounced Man and Wife, Darcy gave a sigh of relief, which made Elizabeth give a little laugh, quickly hidden behind a gloved hand.

Afterwards at the wedding breakfast at Pemberley, Darcy spoke to Anne privately. "Do you truly wish to marry Richard?"

Anne nodded. "I do," she said quietly. "I have

always enjoyed his company, and I wish to be married, if only to live apart from my mother."

Darcy did not know how to ask, but he knew that he must warn her about Richard. "I don't know what sort of husband he will be. There is no harm in him, but if you want children, he may disappoint you."

Anne smiled, "Oh, do not worry. I fully understand where Richard's interests lie. And as long as he is discreet, I will have no complaints."

Darcy's eyes widened, surprised by her perceptiveness.

Anne continued. "I understand your concern. But unlike your Elizabeth, I do not want children. I have no maternal feelings. And I am not romantic. I never have been. All I want is a quiet life, free to do what I will with little interference. I believe our Cousin Richard will do very well as a husband for me."

It was not the sort of marriage Darcy wanted, but he could see the wisdom in it for them. "Then I wish every happiness for both of you, he said finally.

"Just as I do for you and Elizabeth."

Darcy bowed. "Thank you."

As he walked through the crowd of guests to

return to Elizabeth, Darcy considered what Anne had said – that she wanted a simple life, to do what she wished.

Was she any different than Elizabeth?

Elizabeth had not wanted to marry him. She had not wanted to marry anyone, and if it were not for the baby, she would have continued to reject him.

Was he overly confident to think that Elizabeth would one day come to love him as much as he loved her?

He was not a man accustomed to doubts, but he now felt some unease.

He watched as Elizabeth spoke with her sister Jane, Mrs. Bingley now. He knew from Bingley that their plan was to go north to the Lake District for their wedding trip.

Darcy knew that many people considered Jane the beauty of the family with her fair hair and blue eyes, but he found her looks insipid compared to Elizabeth's. Elizabeth was more vibrant, and much more to his taste.

When Elizabeth saw him approach, she smiled at him, and he trusted her smile. She no longer disliked him, but he wanted more from her. He wanted her heart and soul.

He thought of the words of the wedding cere-mony. He had promised to love her, to comfort her, and to honour her all the days of his life. He hoped that ultimately his devotion would be sufficient to win her affection. He did not want her to feel that their circumstances had forced her hand.

Elizabeth reached over for his hand and said in a quiet voice, "How soon can we leave, Mr. Darcy?"

Darcy's heart leapt at the words. "As soon as you wish."

CHAPTER EIGHTEEN

ELIZABETH DECIDED that she liked being Mrs. Darcy very much. Darcy's carriage was nicer than her fathers' and he had an abundance of servants so that there was little she had to do. She was able to change from her wedding dress to travel clothes and promptly climb into a luxurious carriage.

She was married now. She had cried a little when she said good-bye to her father, but he had promised to visit Pemberley for Christmas.

She and Jane had already said their good-byes the day before and managed to separate without tears.

As Elizabeth swayed to the gentle motion of the carriage, she thought of her wedding day. She did not think anything could be more dramatic than

Lady Catherine's appearance, but it had certainly given them a memory never to be forgotten. And if truth be told, it showed her that Darcy's family could be vulgar as well. She needn't be so embarrassed by her mother's antics.

Personally, she was surprised that Colonel Fitzwilliam wanted to marry Anne de Bourgh, but she wished them well.

At another critical point of the ceremony, Mary had sneezed, and Mrs. Bennet had admonished her. Mary had whispered in a tone loud enough to be heard by everyone, "No one can stop a sneeze."

Elizabeth sighed. She was glad that all the fuss was over.

Darcy sat on a cushioned seat across from her. He said, "Are you tired?"

"A little," she confessed. "I did not sleep well last night."

He looked alarmed. "Did you go walking?"

"No, not at all," she assured him. "I only did that twice, and with my door guarded, I did not leave my bedroom."

He nodded. "Good. And you need never worry about that again."

"Thank you," Elizabeth said. "I think I walk more when I am in a new place. Hopefully it won't take long for me to become accustomed to Darcy House as well as Pemberley."

He smiled. "They are both your homes now."

She smiled and it turned into a yawn that she covered with a gloved hand. "Forgive me," she said. She did not want to give him the impression that she found his conversation tedious.

"Nothing to forgive," he said simply and patted his lap. "Why don't you rest your head and sleep?"

"You don't mind?"

"Not at all."

Accordingly, she removed her bonnet, placed it neatly on her seat, and moved over to sit by him. She shifted so her head and shoulders were across his lap. She said again, "you don't mind?"

"Of course not," he said. "I would prefer that you are well rested tonight, and if you sleep, I will entertain myself by admiring your hair and the sweet curve of your dainty ear." He lightly touched her ear as he spoke.

She smiled at the absurdity of the compliment. Darcy continually surprised her. She relaxed, and in a few minutes, she was asleep.

They stopped at an inn that evening and Darcy paid for a meal to be brought up to their room. Elizabeth's new lady's maid helped her dress for bed and changed the sheets, and then Darcy joined her, dressed in a nightshirt and a long silk dressing gown. Elizabeth had met his valet Chetti earlier and thought he was imposing with his rigid posture and exotic attire.

Elizabeth thought Darcy looked handsome in the firelight.

Darcy said, "You are so beautiful." He motioned to her hair and said, "May I?"

"What?"

"Undo your braid."

"Of course."

Darcy stood by her, kissing her lightly as he undid the maid's work. "You have glorious hair."

She reached out to his hair and said, "You do as well," which made him smile. He kissed her until her knees felt weak and she swayed against him.

He gathered her close, kissing her neck and throat. He carefully untied the ribbon at the neck of her gown, and she shivered.

"What is it?" he asked.

She said quietly. "I don't know what to do."

His eyes seemed to blaze as they looked at her with adoration. "Let me show you," he said and slid her gown off one shoulder. "Let me seduce you."

His hand cupped her breast and she leaned toward him, sighing.

He said, "Yes, just like that."

He kissed her deeply and it made her heart race. She felt as if her heart were beating between her legs. As if reading her thoughts, he placed his hand there, over her gown, rubbing gently. He said, "Do you remember what I promised today? *With my body I thee worship.*"

She moaned.

Darcy caught her up in his arms and carried her over to the large four poster bed. He lay her down on the cool cotton sheets and removed his own attire, so he was naked.

His shoulders were broad and his stomach flat. And his male member was large and jutting towards her, reminding her of some of those pictures in his book.

Elizabeth's eyes widened but she did not shrink away as he joined her on the bed. She would be brave and not missish.

He kissed her again, his tongue darting into her mouth, making her gasp and clutch at his bare shoulders, his back. "How I love you," he said.

Elizabeth arched her back, revelling in all the sensations he was creating. Then a familiar queasiness arose in her stomach. "Oh, no," she said and pushed against him.

"What is wrong?" he asked, pulling back.

She wriggled free and climbed off the bed. "I'm so sorry," she said as she frantically searched for a basin. She settled for the chamber pot and knelt on the wooden floor, her stomach heaving as she vomited.

"My poor darling," Darcy said as he knelt beside her. He held her long hair back so it wouldn't fall in her face.

Elizabeth had never been so embarrassed and horrified in her life. Her sickness seemed to take an hour although she knew it was only minutes. "I am so sorry," she repeated when she had finished.

"No," Darcy said. "No apologies. Let me take care of you."

She sat weakly on the side of the bed as he took the pot away from the bed and placed it across the room. He then found a cloth and water to clean her face and hands.

"How do you feel?"

She felt awkward and humiliated, and her stomach was still unsettled. She said, "I don't think I can continue what we were doing earlier."

He nodded. "Let me help you." He retied the

bow at the neckline of her nightgown and then brushed her hair and braided it. His actions were slow and careful. He helped her into the bed and pulled the sheet up to her chin. "Better now?" he asked.

"Yes, but I should –"

"No," he interrupted and tapped his finger on her nose. "No shoulds between us."

"But aren't you disappointed?"

He smiled wryly. "We will be married many years, Elizabeth, and I hope to make love to you thousands of times. And I would like our first time as a married couple to be exactly what you wish. I can wait. Besides, I also remembering promising something about in sickness and in health today."

She smiled at that, grateful that he was so reasonable. She thought that he would dress himself before lying next to her, but instead, he slid beside her, naked. He lay next to her, wrapping his arms around her so they were spooned together.

Elizabeth sighed, finally at peace. Darcy had proven himself in every way. She needn't be afraid of him or their marriage any longer. "I love you," she said quietly.

His arms tightened. "Then that makes everything all right."

OTHER THAN A FEW TIMES, Elizabeth never slept walked again, and for those few occasions, she was safely contained in her bedroom, so there was no upset or confusion. Darcy often teased her, saying that it was because she now slept with him every night; she no longer had any reason to seek him out.

Elizabeth always smiled when he said that and did not argue. She did not know why she had been so drawn to him before they were married. She suspected that it had something to do with his little book combined with her unacknowledged attraction for him.

Some of the servants were surprised that Darcy spent every night naked in her bed. They had begun the tradition on their honeymoon, and he had never departed from it. Apparently, his mother and father, like Mr. and Mrs. Bennet, had maintained separate bedrooms. Elizabeth and Darcy had separate rooms as well, but they never slept apart. They took turns, sleeping together in the two beds – one night in her bedroom, followed by a night in his.

Their first child, a daughter named Jane, was born in late January of the next year. Mrs. Bennet declared that she was a remarkably large and healthy baby considering that she had been born early. Mrs. and Mrs. Bingley had a child that first year as well but two months later.

As for Colonel Fitzwilliam and Anne de Bourgh, they were married quietly and seemed to work well together. Anne found a doctor to help her reduce her laudanum consumption and the Colonel, retired from the military, hired a handsome steward to help him with running Rosings.

Lady Catherine, still bitter that Darcy had married Elizabeth, only lived a few years before dying during one of her tirades with Mr. Collins. The Colonel kept Mr. Collins on as their clergyman.

As for Georgiana and Elizabeth's younger

sisters, all of them eventually married, even Mary, which stunned Mrs. Bennet, who was known to say, "I never thought Mary would find a husband, but he is even plainer than she is, so I suppose it doesn't matter."

Over the years, Darcy read *A Vindication on the Rights of Women* and other radical books that Elizabeth suggested. Elizabeth wore comfortable clothes and learned how to run a large household, becoming well known for her parties and social gatherings.

Although as strong willed, intelligent persons, Darcy and Elizabeth occasionally "locked horns" – to quote the Americans – they were remarkably well matched.

And what happened to the little book of illustrations? It provided them hours of passion and amusement, for one man's meat is another man's poison – even in the bedroom. Darcy found it endearing that after years of marriage and four children, he could still make his beloved wife blush.

He liked to walk up behind her when she was sitting at her desk, writing menus or letters to Jane, and kiss her behind her ear.

Depending on her mood, she might wave him

away, laughing, or suddenly take his cock in her hand.

Either way, he loved her, and she loved him.

And all their servants learned to knock before entering.

Dear Readers:

I hope you enjoyed this sweet sexy story as much as I enjoyed writing it. I'll admit, I felt a little sorry for Mr. Darcy as he tried to be a gentleman while Elizabeth was determined to seduce him.

As with all my various JAFF titles, I enjoy doing the research. For this one, I read about sleep walking and the *Kama Sutra* and its various translations. It was fascinating to see how the book has been characterized and translated in different eras.

And if you would like more of my sexy Darcy stories, please leave a review.

Hester

OTHER HESTER ROSE TITLES

With Darcy at Midnight
Sleeping with Darcy
Darcy's Bit of Muslin
Saved by Darcy
Checkmate Mr. Darcy